DUNESHADOWS

Michael Stevens

Red Arrow Press • Michigan City, Indiana

ACKNOWLEDGEMENTS

Most of this book was written between August of 1989 and March 1990 in Michiana Shores and Chicago. My thanks to the Green Mill and Gallery poets, Gail Van Sickle and Fred and Rosemary Braun of Beverly Shores, Indiana.

Michael Stevens
Michiana Shores, Indiana
September, 1990

Coypright © 1990 by Michael Stevens
All right reserved

Red Arrow Press
3721 Meadow Drive
Michigan City, Indiana 46360

ISBN: 0-9627336-0-1

Typesetting and book layout by:
Laser Type & Graphics Co.

Printed in the United States by MPS, Inc.

CONTENTS

POETRY
SPIRIT OF MACONAQUAH 1
SONG OF THE DUNES 2
THE REMOVAL MEN 4
ON LENINISM IN STEEL TOWN 6
MICHIANA 8
DANCE OF DEATH 10
RUMBLINGS OF OLD MEN 12
SOMBRA AND SOL 15
LA OSCURIDAD DEL FUTURO 17
GENESIS 18
HIDDEN SLUMBER 19
THIS LOVING 20
CAT-DANCE 21
LEG CONTACT 22
EN LA MAÑANA 23
THE COMPETITION 24
I WALKED IN THE GARDEN 26
WHISPERS 28
THE WALKER 30
THE INTERROGATION 32
NETHERSPHERE 33
PAPA 34
HOW MANY MORE 36
COME WITH ME MY CHILD 37

FICTION
SHMELE 40
THE LEARN'D ASTRONOMER 47
THE PREFACE 56

DRAMA
FIFTY-SIXTH WARD, THIRTEENTH PRECINCT 58

FOR JUSTIN AND MARIEL

POETRY

SPIRIT OF MACONAQUAH

In frigid stillness a thousand feet
Dance in spiritual effigy before unblinking moons
I breathe your spirit and raise my hands in wonder

I am your chronicler, your midnight ear,
Your latent scribe and you are calling to me
In tongues once cherished now forgotten

You sing to me in dark waves of splendid ceremony
And I am listening

Pokagon, Tahoma, Miami, Hiawatha
Pottawatomie, Outaüa, Pocantico, Chippewa

Like Segovia, you entrust unto me the task
Of rescuing your glory from the depths of folkloric amusement

I steer inquiry from trivia
From Dillinger, moonshine and dirt-path roadhouses
To the council fire, Little Bear Woman, Maconaquah and beyond

I sing your song
And cast a Shaman's light on your shadows
Where once proud nations knew all things known
Of the sand, the sun, the trees and the water

"I once was a sapling and swayed in the wind,"
You whisper to me in midnight ice
"Now I am an old tree and cannot move about
Speak to them of me, tell my story,
And when the owl calls your name
The great spirit will welcome you"

SONG OF THE DUNES

It's the high, clean wave of windblown dunegrass
bringing forth green scent of eternal childhood summer,
with magic dust in fresh lake air clinging to inside seam
of breathing, each breath almost full but not quite.
Can eyes open any fuller to endless horizon of blue meets hazel
meets auburn shades at dusk but first are distant cries of sea
birds plunging to dead drop tiny spots from high
of cut-bait on thin lines of entrapment gripped by latter day Santiagos

But actually older children hoping for one sure
tug that opens stairway to shoulder shudder then quick
reeling until finally it doesn't seem possible something so
fresh and lifelike emerges from all that dark water
except he'll be staring at me bug eyes if I reeled that quick.
Now quiver and flip onto sun-drenched mahogany deck even
though he's in the net he's all there silver scales
and all looking like God's pristine creation.
Which is nature in its utter simplicity.

So I'll walk up dune hills forever
Until the blood won't wash into my thighs anymore
Until sparrows and bluejays and robins stop calling my song, your song,
the song of alive mankind because you see there are these moments of
clarity not just the true ticks because it's all true but
the clear moments which may be the point of it all.
Where you can see the beauty of life in front of you staring back
Unblinking more than emeralds and rubies all together
Like universal knowledge moments where time stands still
Like well, like naked lunch.

Maybe the evening cool will ease into my conscience
before the reality and I'll think
weren't we sitting around the fire on the beach one night
When they still let you

Gazing into the inner glow like some World's Grandest Fresh
Water Oracle to reveal the warmth and contented knowledge
that everybody is here together; it's okay it's safe
even though we're outside under the blinking stars,
no one back at the house
First hard crackles then more of lazy glow
With unburnt ends falling in a soft thud onto now warm sand
while the hottest hot is white hot
Searing the very core of the thing but no match for blanket
moonlit chill except for that one spot which hurt my eyes
at first but then mesmerized me so that I returned here many years later
Like the forgotten son.

☙

THE REMOVAL MEN

Well I'm here to tell ya that
Ole' Curt Hensen and the boys
climbed into the vehicle one day last year
and headed for the city cause they had a job to do

It didn't matter none that Curt's shirt said Bob over the pocket
and Bob's said Roy and hell,
Roy wore his overalls cause he was late anyway
on account of he left his tools up to the house

Only problem was before they could grab the interstate
they had to stop at Red's Radiator to pick up
that rebuilt carburetor and well, shit,
Red does a good job when he wants to
but he just about drinks twenty four hours a day
and the part wan't ready for'em

So Curt heard that some fella outa Furnessville had one
and they had time, so they headed over
and they got the part but Curt got lost
so they figured they'd stop to eat
When they was through Curt asked an old fella settin there
how far to the interstate extension and the codger said
"Well sir, I don't rightly know, but its so close to five
miles it makes me nervous"

Well they found it and got to the city and located the
building and Roy was making jokes about someone guardin'
the truck but they set to work anyway
Removin' some large stain glass windows from a foyer for cleaning

And the first floor tenant, a widda, by the look of her
came down with cookies and lemonade
And they fed

And she reminded Roy of his dear mother, bless her heart, before she passed
They worked quick and except for Curt losin' his large phillips, which'll turn up anyway, they didn't have problems and them windas was out in no time and they thanked the widda, loaded up and left

Well it seems the widow called the landlord later to tell him it was indeed a pleasure to meet some polite workers for once and he said
"Which workers?"
and she told him and he said "what in God's name are you talking about woman" and, "I'll be right over"

☙

ON LENINISM IN STEEL TOWN

If you want justice in Steel Town you have to wait
The wheels turn slowly
So you reside with those of similar fate
But that's not the point

High above her flowing robe a mural waves
A flag-like relic of bygone days
Beckoning, enticing
"Join With Us," "Forge Our Children's Future," "Reach For Tomorrow" and "Climb Destiny's Way"

Yet here I paused for a discrepancy perceived
A gap between that intended and that received
To my fellow offenders as well
I think not
Irony, indeed

There is something in the glint of the steelworker's eye
A definition of purpose, the inclined glaze of those assembled,
Black, white, hispanic
Equality among people resembled

A slogan whispered from the majestic wall
Long forgotten from another hall
Memories recalled
Streets of fire, rising phoenix-like
No moon for these misbegotten
Shall I remind you, tease you,
A simple phrase
"Workers of the world unite"

It could have worked, they said
First here, if it worked at all
It could change America, or so they thought

Here, in this fiery oasis
Where boiling cauldrons
Seared youth from men's faces
And they said of this jungle
None of my children's places

Yet work they did with pride and purpose
They built this country their strength in surplus
Free and eager to build and grow
Capitalism unchained! No.
Freedom, pure and simple
Lenin's death knell

"Freedom Shrine" a sign declares
As my name is called, amid the stares
How do you plead, her honor's query
Guilty I say
For guilty I am
I was in a hurry

A fine I pay and off I trot
An incentive to obey, excuses for naught
But I am thinking other thoughts

Of freedom and glasnost
Emigration, oppression and solidarnosc
How odd she meets my glance
As I smile and meditate
In this hall of justice
Where Leninism never had a chance

☙

MICHIANA*

There's a place I know from years ago
Where the horses tried to fool ya'
Clip clop on by
Without a glint in their eye
As if they never knew ya'

But those horses heard
What we were thinking
Cross-legged on the floor
That America's changed
To a different game
With peace and love no more

Michiana, glad I found ya'
Pine trees smelling pure
Those days are gone
But my thoughts are warm
Like dunegrass on the shore

There were some of us who refused to go
And others who weren't sure
Most of us just tried to grow
In a country less than pure

Our sins were mild
When the flower child
Put roses in the barrel
But J. Edgar was scared
So he refused to share
The red wine from the bottle

Michiana, glad I found ya'
Pine trees smelling pure
Those days are gone

But my thoughts are warm
Like dunegrass on the shore

We made music then
With Mary and Joan
And others less sincere
I recall those songs
Like yesterday
Instead of twenty years

Some of us forgot the songs
For Reeboks and PCs
And others never saw the light
After ambushing VC
But the spirit's there
And we won't forget
What brought us all to tears
Those horses knew like the rest of us
Our tragedies and fears

Michiana, glad I found ya
Pine trees smelling pure
Those days are gone
But my thoughts are warm
Like dunegrass on the shore

*A song dedicated to folksinger Bob Gibson

DANCE OF DEATH

Dusk shot thin shafts of fading sun into the Medina
Between ancient stone buildings and carpet shops
To witness the pirouette
Which I almost missed out on

It was right after the one eyed Arab wanted to trade me
A Djallabah for Old Ben
My trusty corduroy sport coat
All-weather, all-season, all-world

Ben and I sat sipping tea with the men
The women aren't allowed
Except to tease you
Behind black veils
They could even teach the Victorians a thing or two

I didn't catch the prelude
Because you don't hear a stab
The quick in and out of warm steel in flesh
Unless the bone scrapes
But I caught the main act

He whirled twice into the center of the street
By then he had both sides of the narrow way watching
And the balcony of the hotel above
Where I could sleep and shit in a porcelain hole for $1.50 a night

It wasn't the blood, at least not at first
It was the damndest wild look in his eye
Still haunts me
Then he stumbled over to me and whirled again
Caught Old Ben on the sleave

A liquid arrow shot from dark Morrocan veins
I could even smell his foul breath, until he stumbled away
And nobody did anything

"Equal is justice to equal
Unequal is justice to unequal
Never equate equal with unequal"
Thus spake Zarathustra's champion

☙

RUMBLINGS OF OLD MEN

If you encounter old men sipping mint tea and speaking
Arabic before round tables in the Medina at dusk
Then listen to them
And you will begin to understand

If you hear the splatter of submachinegun fire
And daughters screaming unnatural screams
While half-blind sons dress their wounds
You will glean which way the light at the end of the tunnel is shining

If you sit back in armchair apathy and caress
your platitudes like your family dog then I can assure you
The vulgarity of our time will seep in and suffocate you
Like the mist at Auschwitz

Psalm 24 A psalm of David:
Raise yourselves you gates
Raise yourselves you ancient doors
That the glorious king may come in
Who then is the glorious king?

More directly, though
Who's the gatemaster?

From Galilee to the Negev I have trod and
From Solomon to Hertzl I was cradled
But in childlike wonder I will no longer cower

The Lord spoke unto Moses saying:
Speak with the children of Israel and bid them make fringes
in the corners of their garments throughout their generations
Putting upon the fringe of each corner a thread of blue
And it shall be unto you for a fringe
That ye may look upon it

And remember the commandments of the lord
And this land of yours

Perhaps, but their's alone?
How can those who have known such suffering
Forget so quickly
The collective conscience it seems, like the Yourtzeit candle,
Burns strong and firm
But fades in time, in silence

I have a friend who says God did it as a perverse joke
A means to amuse himself during lulls in history
To place the most sacred spot on earth for three religions
In one tiny enclave
To pit one man against another in suicidal rampage
Some joke

If you stroll quietly among garrissoned kibutzim
You will feel the tension inside your spine and ask yourself
How did an ideal so pure
Become a nightmare in history's time
And you will sense guilt Hitler never felt

"It isn't, my friend!"
"It isn't what?"
"It isn't a nightmare in history's time, only in our time.
In history's time it is like a flyspeck"
"That's a lot of bloodshed for a flyspeck."
"Well, after all, it's a very juicy fly."

If you listen for the cadence of its army
You will swear that you have heard that sound before
Not as faint perhaps, but there indeed
That you have met those cries before
And seen the anguish in a prior horror

All we ask, the one-eyed hero said
Is that you feel Jewish
Then you will do what all Jews do to those in need
You will help

I'm here to help
Stop the killing now
Before history buries us for good

SOMBRA AND SOL

In the late afternoon haze of the Plaza De Toros De Madrid,
As elsewhere,
You have a choice between sombra and sol

Ingress is its own spectacle, a passive march of humanity, upward
"Are most seats the same?"
"Sit down amigo! This is not England."
Tio Pepe seduces me-too quickly-I will pay later

The hoofed ballet of picadores in exquisite prelude
To the unnatural union of warm steel and crimson
Raises a conjurer's dust for Pissaro in the fading sun

Enter a beast, and who hasn't felt the same?
Life and death the object, yet, to others, a game
Unfair! Cry the uninitiated, the unknowing, but not, it seems, the child
Revulsion at carnal conflict being, after all, an acquired sense

The finest silk and satin are no match for nature's shiny
blackness, gleaming with sweat, and the perfect orchestration
of a mountain of flesh in a massive charge

A momentary pause, dedication? homage?
Or perhaps one man's insignificance in the universal plaza
Oppressed with heat, which hovers, ready to choke

In the end it is a quick thrust between muscle and bone
But even here, a momentary flicker, disbelief and only then
"A drawing down of blinds"

Death with a flourish, like death with honor is, alas, death unchanged
Shall we glorify it?
In *MissaSolemnis* extol its beauty?

How shall it serve us?
I introspect at great peril
I risk greater sin than disillusionment
"Alchemy in reverse"- I devalue what is most precious to us

☙

LA OSCURIDAD DEL FUTURO

Encontré una luz
Brillante, gigantesca
En la oscuridad del futuro mío

El origen de mi lustre
Fue la necesidad incesante de saber
En las alcances de mi mente

Cuando los hombres, medio ciegos,
Buscan la verdad, se dice,
Hallan la verdad media

Hallé un viejo,
Sabio, pero triste

I encountered a light
Brillant, gigantic
In the obscurity of my future

The genesis of my lustre
Was the incessant necessity to know
In the reaches of my mind

When half-blind men
Search for the truth, it is said,
They find half truths

I found an old man
Wise but sad

GENESIS

After the first time, during genesis
It was your thin smile of mystery inviting hidden glances
of moonlit softness to come
That sent pleasure cascading down my spine
Measured droplets of joy
Past Atlas
Who had grown weary

Some beauty lies in wait, cautious, yearning to be coaxed,
entreated, beckoned into the halflight
Like the reticent child

Your beauty heralds itself
Here I am
Behold me and marvel
Perfection upon magic stilts
Mysterious finally in its endless depth
Deep, deep into your inner soul

This is natural, unadulterated, naked beauty

I must chide myself and thus prefer to read your thoughts
For if I lift my eyes from the printed page
And gaze into your almond starlights
I will forget all wordly thoughts
And drift into the heavens, in perpetuity

HIDDEN SLUMBER

All in preface, all in prelude
Two thousand years of struggle
And sadness not forgotten
Conspired to steal the warmth of your smile
And failed

When the nightingale alights from hidden slumber
And bougainvillea greet first rays of morning
in a distant symphony, once yours
You open your petals and welcome life's sweet nectar
To stillness only briefly pierced
By a passing train's railsong, at dawn

Athena always leaves one door slightly ajar
For without her mystery what would men do?
Your soft rose light invites me to peek
behind the corner
And to lose myself, finally

THIS LOVING

After a time the wind blew
A soft glow across the valley of her back
Faint drops of nature's mercury
Joined together in tiny tributaries

We were floating on a thin vapor
At one point, I think
Then surging on jet rockets and juice
Hurtling through the galaxy
No afterburners needed here

I dug into you in joint descent
A freefall of warm air and hotter skin
An invitation to Prometheus
Burn me

Now you are silent save the steady
Rise and fall of rosy pearls in the halflight
And I gaze upon divine creation
For what other form inspires
As the symmetry of your slender line
And the supple crescent moon of your curve

Open your eyes Athena, and forever beguile me
With your mystery

CAT-DANCE

Into your wetness I purge my sorrow
Forgotten promises, bygone hope
To emerge again
Renewed breathing, even child-like joy

Your moonlit torso melts into an ecstacy,
Cat-dancing
They always know where they're at
But you took a leap on this one
And I caught you in midair, reaching
Muscle to muscle

Somewhere in another time
You turned to me and giggled in sticky August midnight air
And we conspired under the stars

༄

LEG CONTACT

"Its mostly in leg contact, you see"
And she pursed her lips, deliciously
"When you ride horses they sense
How tight your muscles are
And react to the tension"

How true my dear, I thought, under my breath
While the early evening sun fractured her blond hair
Into autumn brimstone

"Do you like to ride? "
She cast a quick glance backward, the corners of her mouth stretching
I like to ride with you, I silently recanted

"Believe it or not," she called back, as she rode ahead in perfect canter
"I have trouble keeping my balance sometimes
That's why I prefer larger mounts
So I have more to hold onto with my legs"

She's got to be playing with me, I reasoned
And waited for the cool trickle of the nearby brook to refute me
Must be remnants of that Australian frontier wit

"Are you going back," I sighed, "down under soon?"
"Oh yeah, " she replied, "that way I have two summers."
"The winter is beautiful here," I called out
But she didn't hear me
And she sped forward, leaning
Tight hips, hair flowing
Guiding the ebb and flow of that graceful animal
"This," I remarked to the cool moss and the blue jays mating,
"is poetry."

EN LA MAÑANA

En la mañana, por la mañana
Judith will launch another grim-visaged, melancholy journey
That no longer interests anyone, but her

"Going through the motions" is charitable
She's trying to suck life from lifelessness
And God knows she hates sucking

"This is it," she will vow "I am somebody," or some shit like that.
Does she dream this life or is it reality in suspended horror?

Except that when he rolled over
She was ready, as always
He sent lightning through her spine
Which shot out at right angles
While she kept arching
Until she went slack, just one more time

☙

THE COMPETITION

The learned judge sat sternly listening to the evening's
competition and round about round two
Someone detected an odor of unfairness
Seeping from his corner
And the crowd started getting antsy which they do occasionally
But the judge kept bombing with scores for one combatant so
low you had to stoop to see 'em

And I blithely remarked that
This guy had no understanding of the concept of pathos
And they were plotting to lynch the bastard
And some of them were only half-kidding
Because poetry does things to people
Ya know

So he kept right at it and her poems were working magic
But not for him, which was sad
Because he held the keys to the whole show
Ya follow me

And it figured he wouldn't judge well
Because he never heard these poems before
And I had, right?

And sure enough he tipped the scales
And she lost
And some were pissed off

Except that later I realized two things that I hadn't before
And that was first that good poetry has to struggle on its
own to breathe for itself
Like the wrinkled skin of a newborn

And secondly, that this bastard had no legs below both knees
And I asked myself who the fuck did I think I was
questioning his proximity to human pathos?
And it was for the better, as it turned out anyway
And ain't life a goddamn marvel sometimes

☙

I WALKED IN THE GARDEN

I once walked with a mafioso, now deceased,
And admired the roses in his garden

No official summons induced me
It was a polite request, with company
In case I lost my way
Curiosity got the better of me

I found him mixing soil
A man of the earth, apparently
Did I like the practice of law, he asked.
He wore sansabelt slacks
And apologized for any inconvenience,
Loose dirt crumbling submissively
Between his thick fingers

It is good for a man to work the earth by hand occasionally,
he remarked
Sometimes we forget, he said
I blinked

He was, it seems, troubled
He had heard something "unsettling"
Something about him
Something I knew about
And wished I hadn't

I told him the truth
He seemed to respect that
He asked if there was anything I "needed"
Because, he said, I know some people
No thank you was my reply
And he clipped a red rose just below the petal

He thanked me for coming
I remarked on the vitality of his garden
His colleagues showed me out
I turned from their watchful eye
And found the fork in the road

The decision was far less lucrative, as expected,
Yet easier than I thought

༼༽

WHISPERS

There's a dream place
On the other side of Arcadia
Bereft of innocence
Where neon and fog keep company in the night

I could call it entertainment
But they don't so why should I
A mysterious spectacle
Dark bodies gliding silently in and out
Soft smiles, sinister sweet things

Two dozen forlorn souls
Who weren't lucky and never will be
Stare silently into half dollar draws, waiting
Some will wait forever
Companions to the darkness
Lethargic, broke or afraid

A communal toilet dispensing life savers
Essential, if your life is afloat upon a sea of strangers
A brief dispute:
"You keep your mother fuckin' hands off me unless you give me some money"

So what do you think honey?
That's thirty for me, twenty for her and, oh yeah
Two quarters for the machine
Just here with a friend?
That's what they all say, sweetheart
I like your hands
Ya got baby hands
Stick around and watch the show
Your pal will be okay

He's having the time of his life
Which life, I ask
There's only one, sugar.

☙

THE WALKER

If you gaze far away in distant past late afternoon low sun
Through three-quarter shade drawn
Most resting after daywork, daydream or even love

If you strain, search, then close eyes to earth end
Like indian sender first watching smoke
You will find him in steady stride
And glean the clean movement metronome march

I know because I have seen him
Who carries a veil of threadbare human frailty
Like a trailing ghost vapor
Who halts not too often but wrings pity
Pity for those poor, lost solitary souls of creation
Who cannot even pity themselves

Why walk, why stroll, why pace your even stride
Endless block upon endless block
With no apparent final mark
Except perhaps your grasp on lucid sanity

I heard you at life's first cry
And you have been my silent reminder since of imperfection
Or serenity

I grew to look for you despite hideous games of juvenile
executives finely tuning a jugular venal instinct
which you felt only through others' pointed jabs

"Hey retard," they yelled
You who never hurt a living thing
Never uttered a sordid word
Just kept marching the steady march
Through our failures and indiscretions

Like the beacon of all just and good, and forgiving

Your father died a painful academic death
Banished to his own inner Siberia
A misplaced hope in Lenin to blame

Your mother was an angel but, alas, a mortal one
Who could not tap your striding strength
When cancer robbed hers in the night

Your brothers burnt their flames early
Then vanished in the great suburban vacuum
But you kept walking
Through America's mistakes and triumphs

Did you share in the spoils or did your stoic smile
spring from some hidden source, some untapped well-spring
That bathes your psyche to this day
While others seek solace in more transient diversion

"Hey retard"
The pain is too great for those now lost themselves,
Beyond pity
"Cry not for me" is what you really meant
In your silent serenity all those years and, once assured,
You spoke more potent thoughts to greater voices
"Forgive them, they know not what they do"

℘

THE INTERROGATION

He never said "I'm into this business to get laid."
But that's what they said he said
The idea, in any event, is to establish and maintain proximity.
To the thing itself

"Now let's see here, Hmn…" Sergeant Sphinx coughed.
"Papers seem to be in order."
She casually held his erect phallus between her thumb and forefinger.
"What about this altercation in Sector C last year?"

"I didn't do it"

"I understand your stance," she replied.
"Which is to say, we all need a fallback. But this simply
won't do. We have you photographed five meters from the fire."

"I was fine-tuning my sex drive. Runs on heat, you know.
Can't get the damn thing started in winter."

"Try Potent Lotion," she offered.
And the Sergeant let out a sly smile.
"All right, you can zip up. I'll overlook your indiscretion."
She stamped his Red Card.
"You should be more careful, though, the Department for the
Reiteration of Bureaucratic Redundancy has issued tough,
new regulations."

"I'll take my chances, Sarge. But thanks for the tip."
And he disappeared into the night with new determination.

☙

NETHERSPHERE

In the nethersphere, in that half-sensed solitude
Between the levity of my joy
And the severity of my sin
I search for clarity
O elusive gem!
Which enlightens me, ad infinitem

Do the ruminations of his nation
Sound the depths of a man's soul
Or is it rather the manner in which
He interprets his conscience
Which dictates the course of human conduct

If alone I shall realize the
Distant and future patter of our legacy
Then deliver my musings with dispatch
Before the pathos of our time overcomes me,
The human spirit, but a flicker on the lost horizon
And I, like a hazy afternoon of remembered youth,
There, but gone

Shall I be stricken as charged from Zeus himself
or per chance instead,
As the sweet vapor from Olympus on high
Breath deep, inhale the spirit of a thousand ages

A subtle touch will do, a slight crack
In the cherished low door in the wall, I plea
It need not bear the weight of conviction, for now,
Or the certitude of Themisticles' decree

Deliver me with wisdom
And I will kneel on the alter of knowledge
And kiss the lips of eternal truth

PAPA

I met a man in the twilight of his years
Who knew me all my life.
Strong hands, strong back, strong heart,
My mother's father, our patriarch.

An ocean crossed, four generations past,
Songs of hope, a spirit to persist instilled
The ideal good come alive,
The necessity of tragic circumstance.

There are those to whom the words life, labor and love
Fit together like well-meshed gears.
This was such a man.
A natural engineer by his own son's terms
And who knows the father better than the child?

Consistency is a rare jewel in this age
Yet there he was, the two of them in truth
But really one together
Who knew a love of untold depth
And kindness, and tenderness.

"What's the secret," an outsider asked.
"Don't listen to him," she said.
"Do what you want," he returned,
For no idle speaker he.
But in reality their eyes met
And confirmed their life-long pact.

For he who had the courage to let his family live and grow
Let those who must intrude take heed.
A child becomes that which he wants to be.
That is his destiny.

A yearly trek to warmer climes renewed him
One blustery spring morning I found him perusing the news,
Tanned and fit.
The white hairs leaping from within his lumberjack shirt at the neck
Like Hemingway, I thought.
Papa indeed.
Not quite unique, you say.
Ah, but this was in the spring of his 86th.

I saw him swing the sledgehammer three years hence
And then to say "We'll try it one more year."
Before the angel came, with reticence.
Long may the spirit of my Papa endure.

☙

HOW MANY MORE

How many more summers
How many more lace curtain afternoons in the upstairs bedroom
Where you can see the lake
And smell the sand
Blowing free from the hot cement to the pier and back

How many more glides up the long driveway in the family car
Toward the big garage with the whitewashed wall
And the homemade benches inside
The wall we used to play pinners on, and on
Into the fall, when you had skin cream ready for tiny chapped hands
Rubbed raw in the wind

How many dinners to come
How many chicken and mashed potato happy moments
Glasses tinkling on the huge dining room table
And chocolate cake from the secret recipe
Like a lost scene from Ibsen

Will there be many more soft spring evenings
Up the long staircase
Angled, not winding
No surprises around the corner
Solid, dependable, in other words

When will I no longer find you in the morning
Relaxing in your bath
The silver-backed hand mirror resting on your dressing table
And the round cushion, inside the round chair, with no back
Waiting for you to finish
Your morning of elegance
In the twilight of your years

COME WITH ME MY CHILD

Awaken, and come with me my child
To taste the breeze flowing through the sugar maple
On this warm August morning when the dew has fallen

We will build sand castles with firm towers
Garrisoned and anchored against the forces of evil
So you may safely ascend your sturdy ladder
And swing for the blue sky

I stand ready to guide you, as you need me, or not
But only softly, for the heights must be your own
And when you jump, for one day you surely will,
I will watch you soar as the eagle gazes upon its young

Come with me my child and we shall behold regal auburn majesty,
A blaze descending at dusk across a sea
You will point to tiny towers as a far away monopoly kingdom,
First illuminated, then faint beyond the water

We will dig to China and I will strengthen your walls
As your round face brushes against the warm sand

We shall mount stallions together, in time
For it is in your blood as well to race faster and leap higher
I sense it

Come with me my child and we shall explore Riverviews of the
mind on rainy afternoons
Then listen to the grudging crackle of the first fire
As the snow falls gently on our roof
I shall warn you not to sit too close, but then we will inch
up together, eager for its silent warmth
And when you inquire of me and brave those thoughts to which
only you and Teddy are privy I will be truthful and wise

For those more insightful than I long ago remarked
that to know and love another human being is the root of all wisdom

So awaken my child and come with me
Our days together are but a speck in the distant constellations
But to me they are as luminous as a thousand suns

☙

FICTION

SHMELE

Salomon Trifkovich had reached the point where he had finally had it with the critics. He had lain awake the previous night trying to reconcile a dilemma that could only occupy an artist's mind. The sole product of his nocturnal labor was a splitting headache. Now as he sat slowly stirring his morning coffee with the flat stirrer he reserved for such occasions, he scanned the lake from his 30th floor dining room view and realized that they had once again, done it to him. That was the only route which promised even a hint of emotional salvation. Equalibrium was totally out of the question, at least before lunch, when he could hope for renewed clarity. He had at first the prior evening, cursed the existence of a moral imperative but realized later that it was nothing categorical which plagued him. Rather, as he turned the stirrer between his thumb and forefinger and watched the drops of coffee slide with each turn, it was quite clearly, a case of "epiphenomenon." He had only a passing familiarity with the concept, but he knew its basic premise as this: we are all observers of and subject to, phenomena; those events which occur around us and which are, undoubtedly genuine. Yet, clinging to the underbelly of these actual events like some intellectual parasite are actually phenomena of phenomena, or epiphenomena. These epiphenomena are merely reactions to phenomena, they aren't the real thing. They aren't genuine. They rely for their luminescense on the obviousness of the actual article. When a person perceives something as obviously genuine as his work, Trifkovich reasoned to himself, it is normal that he would perceive a reaction within himself as well.

The problem now, however, was that the power of his stroke was being lost in the onslaught of expert reaction to his work. What the public was now perceiving as his work was actually reaction to his work. They perceived the epiphenonemal only and in his case, that meant the reaction of "experts." That demeaned his art. Yes, the experts, he concluded, were in reality *epiphenomenum parasiticus*. They were choking him with their praise and his passion for work was dying. The award he would receive that evening which he would soon ready himself for (had he told Gregor to bring the car around at six or seven?) would only encourage suffocation. Triflcovich glanced at a giant block of ice being slowly fractured by the invisible undertow and suddenly had to confess to himself that it had not always been like this. He watched the naked trees brace themselves for one icy flurry after another and wondered why it was always days like this that gave him his most vivid recollections of his youth.

As a young man growing up, painting had been as much a matter of necessity for him as for those his age who had to give up idle pursuits to go to work and support families and toil at daylong jobs they disliked. At the time he was barely twenty and wasn't married. He, his parents and his two older sisters had left their small village two years before the invasion and made their way to Paris before embarking for America. Salomon stayed and started painting immediately. He had had some informal training, mostly on his brush technique as a youth, but his parents, who had some money but were not wealthy, preferred that he spend his spare time learning English, so that he could be a businessman in America. Salomon decided as soon as he saw Paris that it was the most beautiful city he had ever seen and obviously he had to stay in this place and paint. The symmetry of the avenues captivated him. So did the buildings themselves. His parents were heartbroken when he told them of his decision to stay, but his sisters understood. They kissed him tearfully goodbye one morning on the Rue St. George and made him promise to write. His father, who never liked to display emotion, shrugged his shoulders, gave him some money, and wished him well. His mother of course was beside herself. She refused to acknowledge the fact that he was even capable of dealing with the world on his own, particularly in this strange place where too many women eyed her son on the street. She begged him to come with them, or at least follow later when they had made a home in New York USA (she described it that way). Salomon was very much affected by this display on his mother's part. Years later when he described this tearful scene to his friend the Earl of Winthrop, his companion replied that any act requiring real courage results in a heartbroken mother.

Artistically and professionally, there is no question that in retrospect, the timing of Trifkovich's appearance in Paris that winter was fortuitous for two reasons. First, there was at that time in Paris, indeed in New York as well, a general degree of disillusionment which began to be evidenced in the work of certain young painters of the time, some of whom Salomon Trifkovich or simply, Shmele, as he would eventually be known, began to meet almost immediately. Secondly, in a small laboratory in New Jersey, a revolutionary product was being discovered which would soon have an impact on American artistic tastes that no one could have imagined at the time.

After his family departed Shmele measured what little money his father had given him and took a small room in Montmarte above an English Freudian with occasional Hegalian tendencies. He sought work and found it almost immediately as a waiter in a local cafe. His French was abominable, but the owner liked him and knew he would work for next to nothing. The painter was thankful for the work and saved whatever he could each week toward the purchase of materials. He looked forward to the chance to practice his art and toyed with the idea of painting for nothing. His efforts to obtain a genuine commission had gone unrewarded for several months and he was seriously wondering whether to abandon his plan and join his family in America when one night into the cafe walked a group of loud and drunk young boulevardiers.

Shmele's first reaction would have been to ignore them. His months as a Parisiene waiter had not been uninstructional. However, when he noticed the enamel under the nails of the first young man to approach as well as the tiny specks of paint near the crease of his neck, Trifkovich knew who he was dealing with. The young man was not as drunk as the others and he saw in Shmele's eye in an instant the kindred spirit that many men are afraid to recognize in other men; or perhaps they simply mistake it. The young man politely asked Shmele for a bottle of wine for his entourage, and he obliged him. By the end of the evening, the others had gone and only he and the young man were still drinking. The artist's name was Phillipe and he explained the philosophy of his work on into the evening, long after the cafe closed and the two friends had withdrawn to a small outside table, an empty bottle between them.

Painting, Phillipe said, had disintegrated into a mere expression of societal decadence. Baseboard work had become haphazard. Interior walls and ceilings exhibited nothing but brush strokes of the talentless fools who painted them. Window trim was atrocious. Soffits and eves, for which exterior European painting was most well known, had been regulated to the uninitiated and the general degree of craftsmanship had experienced such a total decline that Phillipe and his associates or, as they were known professionally, Phillipe and Associates, had come to a final, inevitable conclusion; that painters should no longer charge for their work in the private sector. Municipal projects were of course excluded from this artistic statement for obvious reasons and this he confided, was in fact how Phillipe could maintain himself in the style to which he had grown accustomed. This particular school of thought, he went on, had come to be known as Nadaism and it was gaining momentum in Paris as well as New York. It was such a novel ideal that it had enhanced Phillipe's reputation in both cities. As a matter of fact, he had recently purchased a third truck and was in the process of hiring another crew. He looked Shmele in the eye for several seconds and said, "I knew you painted as soon as I saw you, but let me ask you this, Do you paint to please others or to please yourself?'" Shmele gazed toward the Gare St. Lazare down the street and replied, "I am a painter. I must paint." Phillipe looked at him and asked, "Then why are you a waiter?" Trifkovich replied "I could never cease to be what I am. You know why I wait on tables." Years later Shmele would readily acknowledge that evening as the turning point, but refused to concede that it was really the 1938 Beaujolais they were drinking as Phillipe told it, and not Rothchild. Phillipe offered him a position and Shmele's waiting days were over.

He quickly found himself developing a large following as the third man in Phillipe's crew and recognized the simplicty of Nadaism. Since Phillipe charged his private clients nothing, his reputation spread throughout Paris. The strength of that reputation allowed for greater artistic freedom and encouraged more municipal commissions. In those early days, the dining hall of Madame Fuquet particularly, and the Pissoir Rue de Foucanet were generally considered too radical and lacking in breath and contrast. Today, they are conceded to be two of the finest Nadist examples remaining. Yet even as his reputation for baseboard detail, eve work and window sashes grew and his association with Phillipe became mutually profitable, Shmele began to realize that Nadaism was a fad, a simple device to promote the reputation of its practitioners. Three factors caused Trifkovich to reconsider and finally, after two years, jettison, his allegiance to Nadaism and Phillipe. The Nadists were overly concerned with detail and thought themselves more important than their art. Secondly, war and the occupation in particular had removed the eminence of oil base paint and the materials available to Trifkovich were inferior and too costly to justify painting for nothing. Lastly, Trikovich had developed lower back pain from stooping at low windows. He severed his business relationship with Phillipe and began to take commissions on his own.

His transition was not easy. In the spring of 1943, his reputation as a Nadist was eliciting many requests for work, but when his new customers learned he was no longer painting simply for artistic expression the response was less favorable. The Germans of course had their own ideas about house painting and a civil commission for Shmele was out of the question for the time being. He also knew Paris was becoming more dangerous for him everyday. His family was safe in New York, his father had obtained work and he began to make plans to come to America. His first solo commission delayed that journey.

The widow Madame Cyril Du Rochmaneaux was a woman to be reckoned with, especially during the Occupation. She was one-quarter Jewish but went to great pains to hide this fact. She considered herself to be within the inner circle of society, but most of those who cared judged her position to be peripheral. There was notice of her considerable wealth, however, including a large apartment near the Tuilleries which was in need of decorating. Shmele's first meeting with her was tumultuous. First she asked him to quote a fee for the boudoir which he did, indicating he must be paid first with materials extra. Then she told him she wanted the whole apartment done with wall treatments for the original boudoir cost plus a price fixe for materials. Shmele took her to be deranged and stomped out. He needed the money however, and accepting the commission began the work the next day.

Halfway through the project he suddenly realized he would not have enough paint to finish. He had two rooms left and decided on a bold stroke. First he washed the old walls and ceiling with a special cleaning solution he had perfected himself, the most important ingredient of which was Russian vodka. Then he painted a series of vertical lines in lighter and lighter shades of his base on only one wall of each room, continuing up to the ceiling. He signed his name at the bottom near the unpainted baseboard.

The Widow was beside herself. She had returned home in the late afternoon to be ushered into this artistic debacle by one of her servants and promptly fainted. She would remain bedridden for days. Shmele hastily drew his dropcloths together and left without cleaning his brushes. The rest, of course, was really a reflection of art itself. The Widow's acquaintances on hearing that she had suddenly taken ill descended upon her, hoping for a legacy. Each fell over the other in an effort to comfort her in what was taken to be her approaching last hours. She could not speak of Shmele's artistry for fear of ridicule. Even if she had, she lacked the strength to do so. Slowly first, then like a grass fire spreading itself quickly and easily however, the word began to circulate even among proper society that the widow had illustrated something really quite different in her dining room and parlor. It was unconventional. It was unique, it was well, quite unlike anything to date. It was clearly Anti-Nadist. It was not neat. It was not European. It bespoke something fresh and different. It was the work of a young painter who had not heretofore developed an identify or following of his own. The city and its people were tired, and this new idea bathed and revived the senses.

Shmele's reputation eclipsed itself continually in the months that followed. The Widow's apartment spawned a list of important commissions which grew quickly as did his fortune and reputation.

His work became even more unconventional with each new project at the delight of his patrons. The Widow recovered briefly and was finally accepted into the inner realm by the those who had sought to keep her out of for so long. She died shortly after Liberation, but her revised will included a generous bequest to Shmele, who was by then the foremost decorator in the city. He had finally settled on a technique which involved varying degrees of viscosity in his paint from top to bottom-very thick at the bottom with a great deal of texture with an ascending thinness, almost as if the paint were smeared on without concern for pleasure. The results, it was agreed, however, were breathtaking.

In the three years that followed, he was copied extensively by a number of younger painters, the most successful of these being Jean Claude Les and the Englishman, Alistair Moore. Les was quite serious in his own way, preferring to work only in his studio in Montmarte showing his assistants what to create and seeing no one else. Passionate Parisians insisted on one of these three giants, Les, Shmele or Moore, or they would have no one to decorate for them. It became fasionable in certain literary circles to debate the relative merits of these painters. L.E. Abogodow finally put the controversy to rest when he described Shmele as certainly the foremost living representative, indeed the father, of the Shmearkist school of painting, as it had come to be known. It was subsequently revealed that the young Frenchman Les and the Englishman Moore were actually the same person.

As his reputation grew, Shmele began to paint less and lecture more and soon his work brought him to America. He had visited with his family several times in New York prior to leaving Europe and on one such trip, he ventured to New Jersey where a chemist friend introduced him to a new product that he was working with in his lab, which had been invented just before America's entry into the war. It was called latex and could be diluted to liquid form with water to increase its volume.

Shmele had been looking for some time for a cheaper non-toxic paint that covered well but could be maintained at various degrees of density. The ready availability of this product in America had brought him to the U.S. for good and eventually to Chicago in the early 1950s. In Chicago, he had hired on a young half-breed Indian alcoholic who possessed real talent for exterior brush work and could perform miracles when he chose too. His name was Earl Crews, and Shmele found him painting a wooden gutter one day on one of the few old Victorian houses left near Shmele's apartment. The two began talking and became fast friends. Crews lived in a flophouse on Winthrop Avenue near Wilson and was known as the Earl of Winthrop to his acquaintances, most of whom he owed money to at one time or another. His existence was marginal, but the Earl knew a good paint job when he saw it. He also believed that American house painting, once an art, was fading because of a lack of imagination. "Every damn thing is a copy of somethin' else," he would complain to Shmele when they would occasionally share a beer together after a job was finished. The Earl was born and raised in New Mexico and he thought it was about time that the Southwestern and Indian influence was seen in Chicago. "Hell, I tried it myself once on a big stucco number way up north," he told Shmele "but they threw me out while my brushes were still wet." Eventually he drank more than he painted and Shmele let him go. He heard from someone else that Earl fell from a two-story ladder one afternoon several years later and died.

These reflections had quitely replaced the pain that Trifkovich felt earlier and he was relieved. Outside it was still cold, but he could tell the wind had dropped. An answer to one of his prior questions suddenly occurred to him as he sat with his coffee surveying the view. If the critics were true parasites, then they could not help the fact that Shmele's work was the object of their attention and the force which drew them was genuine, no matter how they misunderstood. He liked that reasoning, and the thin veneer of uncertainty which had plagued him earlier began to evaporate. He placed his coffee cup and stirrer in the sink and prepared to draw his bath.

༄

THE LEARN'D ASTRONOMER

It was the enormity of the place, and the massive celestial ceiling that first struck me when Dad, Bob and I walked into the lecture hall that late winter morning a generation ago to be enlightened on a subject I knew nothing about. It was my older brother's idea and that's the best thing about having an older brother. You succumb blindly to all kinds of schemes and entrust yourself without having to examine the exigencies of the enterprise. You just do it because if he thought of it it's the thing to do and that's all there is to it. I felt that way about most things we did together growing up. It is equally as true that children live vicariously through others at times as adults through their own offspring, years later. One afternoon I watched my brother hit a home run over the fence in a Little League game and couldn't believe the ball kept going in a steady line until the left fielder just stopped running and watched. It wasn't a long home run but damn it, he actually hit one over the fence. This was in the first Little League stadium in our town that had an outfield fence, a belated recognition that if these parents wanted their embryo doctors, lawyers, engineers, accountants and landscape architects to think like major leaguers they better provide a real fenced in stadium and not merely a backstop fronting acres of grass that alcoholic park district workers complained about mowing.

Anyway this was astronomy not baseball but who could blame me for viewing the world in baseball terms because that's all we did during the season. The trip downtown just prior to spring training that year actually had a dual purpose. The first stop was at a special model railroad toy store. Not a store that also sold railroad items or that carried a large selection. This was a store devoted exclusively to model railroad paraphernalia. My father saw it nestled under the el tracks one evening as my parents drove downtown for one of their occasional nights out when they would bring back tiny umbrellas from exotic drinks for my sister. Dad probably said something like, "Well, what do you know." His engineer mind had an economy of speech in those days . He would think about most things and only speak at the tail end of his thought, thus assuming that the listener was reading his thoughts and only needed the final few words to complete the sentence. My mother probably said in a sort of a distracted way "What's that, dear?" but kept looking out her window with neither of them speaking further.

Our train set was somewhat modest compared to my cousin's which was permanently affixed to a large board in his basement. Ours was portable, thus allowing its removal if my mother scheduled one of those cousins luncheons where geriatric women would smile at me with a mouth full of food, large fatty deposits under their biceps, and ask "Who am I, honey? Do you know which aunt I am?" In the days before I developed a studied indifference I once responded to one, "Oh I don't know, Aunt Lizzy?" "Aunt Izzie!" she shrieked in laughter. "Aunt Izzie!" and proceeded to share this faux pas with her cohorts. "No,"I protested, "Aunt Lizzy! Aunt Lizzy!"She suddenly lowered her demeanor and remarked seriously, "Oh no honey, Aunt Lizzy has been dead for many years."

We purchased large corner sections of track at the railroad store. They had built in wooden trestles and obviated the need for inserting the many smaller corner pieces with plastic supports we were currently using. Then we walked over to the Academy of Sciences auditorium.

Bob had heard about this lecture from none other than Arthur Carlson himself. In the teaming fertile petrie dish which was the great suburban educational experiment there were numerous wunderkind vying for the role of Mr. Science. There was no official competition but it was generally accepted in our school that Carlson had ascended to the throne in sixth grade with his now legendary use of amoebic parasites in sanitation disposal at the annual science fair. He further solidified his position the following year with an extensive examination of the ability of embryonic fluid to retard secondary infection of the feline genitals, although some controversy was raised as to where and how the fluid was obtained with fingers pointing to his uncle, the eminent OB-GYN with offices downtown and the suburbs. The only serious competition that year came from a thoroughly unprofessional colleague whose father was a butcher. This project consisted of simply displaying the entire digestive system of a calf on a sheet of plastic with various cardboard arrows pointing to salient features. The judges were unimpressed but this carnal display was certainly the most well attended project in the room.

It was Carlson who had informed my brother in the strictest confidence that a great astronomer would be speaking on such and such a date at the Academy downtown as if the Academy was Carlson's second home and my brother had the slightest interest in astronomy which he didn't but being struck by the honor of the invitation suggested to my father that we attend anyway. Because after all, I now know Hegel was right, you only know what you know.

There is a dignity to serious scientific inquiry that transcends time. And perhaps that one morning, in a real brush with academia in its grandest posture I sensed that there was more to knowledge than reading suggested curricula, that there was more to education than listening to another's thoughts and that there is a felt experience of wisdom which exceeds even physical pleasure when one can be altered in an intellectual sense.

The auditorium began to fill as we seated ourselves. Bob mentioned to Dad that maybe we should have brought along a small section of steel track to make sure the corner pieces were the same gauge but Dad said not to worry because he thought they were the same and we could always exchange them. You could exchange everything in those days. Bob went to the washroom for a minute and while he was gone the crowd grew quiet and the President of the academy stepped to the podium to introduce the speaker.

His remarks were brief but as he spoke I noticed a portly young man with glasses walking up the aisle toward us and realized it was Carlson. I had only seen him once or twice but knew who he was. I became concered that Bob might experience a loss of face if our presence was not somehow acknowledged so I stood up. "Arthur" I expelled in a burst of air, and the young man stopped in his tracks. He was only two years older but peered at me in a somewhat arrogant fashion from behind his glasses. "Do I know you?" he asked. My father looked at me. "Well no. But you know my brother Bob. I saw your exhibit at the fair." I extended my hand. He shook it with an air of uncertainty. "Bob?" he faltered. "Please help me. Have we met before? What fair?" he probed. "The science fair," I replied and my heart sank. Perhaps he really didn't know my brother or had forgotten the invitation he extended. "Look here," the young man rejoined. "I don't think I know you and my name isn't Arthur." I suddenly realized my error but actually felt better about it. "You're not Arthur?" and I continued to pump his hand. "No, I'm not," he replied. "Well… it's good to see you anyway," and the young man nodded and smiled. Then he walked away. I looked at Dad. "I thought that was Arthur." He nodded. "Bob must have two friends named Arthur." Bob returned and the applause began as the speaker made his way to the podium.

He was an ashen man who walked slowly with a cane, and had a minor hunchback which caused one end of his limp grey suit jacket to hang lower than the other. A disheveled shock of white hair leaped from behind his forehead above thick, bushy grey eyebrows.

The mood in the auditorium may have been affected somewhat from the initial shock at his appearance by those who had never seen him but any hesitation soon gave way to the thunderous applause of those who recognized him as truly one of the giants of modern day astronomy. He rested his cane on the corner of the dais, adjusted the microphone and gripped both sides with thin, hairy hands.

Before he could speak a minor commotion arose directly in back of us. I may have heard it at first but my curiosity was peeked by now and I was anxious to hear great utterances from the podium. I therefore lacked actual notice of the intruder until he was quite close.

It is axiomatic that men of science are indifferent to human economic disparity. More than one marginal street person in a university town has been mistaken for an eminent faculty member, making his way down the boulevard lost in vigorous thought mumbling to himself. In a select few academic venues this type of behavior is even encouraged with appropriate precautions made for limited access of automobiles to the campus to prevent collisions with scholarly pedestrians. The value of these sojourns cannot be minimized in the advancement of academic thought. However, the line can usually be drawn with regard to human hygiene. The eminent physics professor, no matter how distant his contemplation, will normally find some pleasure in soap and water on a regular basis. A soul who is simply lost, on the other hand, having slipped through the societal fabric, will not be so lucky.

I mention all this because it was an odor which preceded the intruder into the lecture hall that morning of the kind which prompts looks of alarm giving way to social resignation by the offended parties. He was not a bum, not exactly, because he expressed a look that indicated he did not have to be there that morning however, his appearance lacked dignity. He was of medium height but ghastly thin and probably hadn't eaten in days.His unshaven face was as stark as the bleak winter morning.His unkempt black hair had long grey streaks and was matted down in different directions. His checkered red shirt was buttoned at the neck and tucked into oversized brown pants tied at the waist with a dirty piece of rope.He wore dusty black shoes with no socks and mumbled to himself as he made his way past us looking for a seat. Dad looked at him but said nothing. Bob and I were fascinated with his appearance despite the foul smell. People like this didn't live in the suburbs. They didn't have afternoons of culture followed by ice cream and the long ride home and they certainly didn't have model train layouts in their basements.

He found a seat two rows down to the right which was close enough for me to look at him but far enough so that we didn't have to smell him. Dad noticed my intense expression and was probably caught between the educational aspects of the experience for his sons and the infringement which this belated entrance represented. "Don't stare, Tommy," he remarked, and I looked at my father. "He probably is just looking for a warm place to sit."

But by this time the speaker was talking, not in a crisp, booming, astronomical delivery but instead in a rather wispy low breathed cry. He spoke of "general propositions" and "feigned indifference" to so and so and such and such and if I hadn't read on the program that his subject was black holes I couldn't really have said he was talking about astronomy and physics at all. But then the wispiness began to fade into spurts of excitement as his long, hairy hands hugged the dais. The lights had dimmed and he was now drawing circles on the overhead projector, concentric circles, centrifugal circles, centripedal circles and all kinds of scientific descriptions began to spew forth. He spoke of "rips in the fabric of space and "unimaginable gravitational forces" stemming from "rapidly pulsing cosmic migrations."

Here was a man, I now concluded, who clearly enjoyed his subject, who thrived on scientific research and obviously knew his stuff. I was pleased with the setting all at once and was glad Carlson, wherever he was in that enraptured crowd of several hundred, had extended the invitation to Bob and wasn't this something else that Bob was onto that was more fun than water balloons from the roof or putting a chicken bone in the old widow's mailbox, but suddenly we heard something very disturbing. It came from the direction of the bum, the homeless vagrant or whatever he was because there in the midst of this hall of science, this bastion of academic enlightenment, he wasn't only sleeping, he was snoring, snoring loudly. Even Dad, who had been listening intently, looked perturbed then and the others began to look up, some shaking their heads, others glaring in his direction. Finally after about thirty seconds which seemed longer a burly man in a blue three piece suit whose stomach looked like it was going to burst through his vest buttons leaned over and shook the bum out of it. The vagrant opened his eyes with a start and then gazed up at his accoster but said nothing. The burly fellow glared at him with his hand still on the bum's shoulder. At that point the bum turned his head slowly to his left shoulder and as the other began to release his grip I swear I saw a sly smile on the bum's face and I thought you've got a lot of nerve buddy sleeping in a place like this with a world renowned expert at the podium.

The speaker was unfazed by any of this and probably didn't even hear the altercation because he was moving at a greater clip with his concentric circles on the overhead projector and drawing lines in and drawing lines out and the thought occurred to me maybe he was oblivious to the audience except he went on for only a few more minutes and then the lights went on to a thunderous ovation and he was through.

I glanced over to the intruder, who had almost spoiled it for everyone, and noticed that even though he wasn't clapping at least he was awake and was looking down to the podium. After the applause subsided the speaker remained at the dais, although by now he had relaxed his iron grip, and the President of the Academy bounded up the steps and stood there smiling with the speaker and I think somebody even took a picture. The President made a gesture with his hands and the applause subsided as he leaned toward the microphone. "I'm sure we all wish to thank the Professor for his cogent presentation here this afternoon. We only have a few minutes but I trust the Professor would be happy to entertain a few questions."

I thought hard about it quickly. Maybe, just maybe I could think of something that wouldn't sound too foolish but would still show I was interested. I know Dad would be proud of me. Bob was looking for his coat in back of his seat and while I thought about all of this the questions started coming from the front and I figured well, maybe I'll read up on black holes and if we go to another lecture I'll be ready because after all, Dad and Bob and I were practically regulars at this point. I heard the President say they had time for one more and suddenly Dad told Bob to sit down for a second and I looked over and lo and behold there was the bum with his hand in the air about to be recognized. My heart took two quick jumps because I knew I was going to witness a public embarrassment. Why would they even recognize him, I wondered. Why give the guy the time of day, especially after that stunt he pulled in the middle of the lecture. But I realized serious science shouldn't suffer from emotional aspects like that and I heard the President say, "Yes sir, near the top," and saw the motion of his arm in acknowledgment.

And from that cloaked and matted grey body and stubbled face came a voice quite different than I expected. It started out from his very insides like a volcano and gathered strength on its way up until he expelled air in a great rush but not out of control and not too loud.

"Do I understand correctly Doctor, that you attribute the existence of rapidly pulsing cosmic radio waves to rotating neutron stars with an individual mass approximately that of the sun?"

The stirring in the crowd faded quickly as his voice dropped at the tail end of the question.

The Professor peered up a moment, returned his hairy hands to the dais, leaned toward the microphone and said, "Yes, that is correct."

The grey face responded and this time the voice was stronger. "Would you agree also Doctor, that the existance of these pulsars, if that indeed is what we shall call them, is only possible through the existence of neutron stars, which can only consist of densely packed neutrons in an atomic nucleus with unusual mass/circumference ratios?"

At this juncture the room had grown almost silent. Several rows in front I noticed a look of extreme concern on the face of a distinguished looking aged man with a white beard.

The Professor thought a moment and suddenly his voice quivered slightly, "Well, primarily yes... I suppose I would not take issue with that notion."

And the response from this inquirer, this homeless bum, this vagrant whoever he was, at this point showed no mercy. "Well then wouldn't you agree," he exploded from his perch high above the podium, "that due to the very gravitational influence on nearby matter that is present, that all energy could be extracted from the black hole if it were rotating through superradiance? And therefore that those waves in the vicinity of the black hole would be *amplified* or thrown off rather than *absorbed,* as you erroneously postulate, by the rotating black hole? And therefore what I am suggesting to you, Doctor, is that the initial premise that you presented to us this afternoon is, shall we say, questionable?"

The Professor had been listening but knew the conclusion the man had been heading for even before it occurred to the others and thus was almost in a blank state, like some lump of weary celestial matter, spinning silently and infinately toward a distant galaxy. He was more resigned than anything else when he simply said, "Yes, I suppose so, if you state it in that fashion" and his voice trailed off.

There was silence as the audience digested the exchange and some began to peer up from the first rows at the inquirer. But he was already moving toward the aisle and on his way out and this time the usher at the door, who it turned out was Arthur Carlson himself, the real one, held the door open for him, because Carlson could smell at that moment, like all good scientists, which way the research money was drifting.

And as the crowd filed out there was an odd feeling in the air, and somebody mentioned something about reviewing the program committee's budget for the following year. And we walked out with the rest of them and Dad told Bob on the way home to check the gauge of the track to make sure it was the right size as our new corner pieces and we never did attend any other lectures at the Academy.

☙

DRAMA

THE PREFACE

One could not hope to undertake a work of this scope without the support and devotion of an army of supporters and it is this legion in the literary shadows to whom this work is dedicated. To the cafe hostess who provided me uncounted cups of stiff cocoa after long solitary morning walks spent formulating the basic theme of this text to the tender of the neighborhood kiosk where I purchased The Times each evening and thus withdrew from the rigors of this exercise I am eternally grateful.

Languishing as I have for almost a decade on this work and then to produce a scant two hundred pages made me seriously reconsider this enterprise more than once. Nevertheless I have written this book because certain things simply had to be said. Certain misconceptions had to be pointed out. No one to my knowledge has previously attempted to document paleontologically the emergence of the pendulous penis in hominid phylogeny. The data verifying the onset of frontal to frontal copulation has been likewise neglected. Yet, my overall purpose is broader. I seek to attack the very complacency which has thus far hindered serious inquiry into the paleontological evolution of the very cradle of one of man's most important organs. It is not an easy journey. It is to those readers who are willing to set aside prior prejudice and examine the material in a close, almost revolutionary, albeit unique fashion, to whom I dedicate my efforts.

A manuscript, like a molehair, can be a tedious thing, and I was extremely fortunate to have the services of Mrs. Edith Teeburgen, as always, as my faithful transcriber and confidante in the course of my labors. Only once did she falter in her ability to deftly and cogently make sense of my incoherent ramblings, especially after those long walks, and I certainly cannot blame her for the one incident which I will forthwith make no further reference to except to emphatically state again it was not I who left the instrument plugged in causing it to overheat. In any event her typing, as usual, was flawless and shows no evidence of the difficult circumstances under which she labored. I hope and trust her response to the linament treatments is quick and satisfactory. Mrs. Teeburgen's dogged determination on a machine which turned out to be the best bargain at the Clivebourne estate sale leads me to dedicate all that follows to her.

To my colleague and mentor, the late Professor E.C. Beckwith, I am eternally indebted for his kind words and cogent analysis, his admonition not to lose sleep over the abnormal slope of the Transval Ischia and his correct suggestion that the material may have warped slightly due to an initial immersion in saline solution by a now banished over-anxious graduate student named Dart, instead of any pathological abnormality. To Dr. Gunther Schloop, now of the Institute for Impotent Research but then of the Archive Du Homme Moderne in Lyon, my thanks for access to the Velterein remains, fragmentary though they be. A colleague who reviewed this manuscript asked point blank how I could suspend an entire thesis on a bone fragment no bigger than a child's arm and it occurred to me that this is precisely the type of narrow thinking which has prevented us from grappling with the pendulous penis question to date and I will withhold his name to avoid professional embarassment.

F.R. Codgehunt of the Neanderthal Museum and Children's Park in Winfordshire graciously granted me access to the very lifelike reconstructions which served as a basis for some of the illustrations accompanying the text. I only regret that the local council took the unenlightened view that it did in response to the graphics and hope that parents in the area will take their children outside the district to view the finished product. I cast this treatise afloat with F.R. "Choppy" Codgehunt in mind.

Finally, I wish to express my thanks to my friends and colleagues who have "taken up the slack" during my enforced exile and while in the latter case I sensed no reticence on the issue of compensation the sacrifice on the former was considerable and I dedicate this book to them.

A.A. Worthington
Sneedscliffe, Harrow
12 March 1988

FIFTY SIXTH WARD, THIRTEENTH PRECINCT

SCENE ONE - MORNING

The dingy, basement meeting room of a high-rise housing project in Chicago. The early light from the eye-level windows is partially blocked by the two large voting machines that were delivered two days earlier and have remained shuttered. To the left of the machines is a collapsible wooden table and five metal folding chairs. On top of the table are several clipboards with registration lists, an old coffee pot, a closed box of sweet rolls and a stack of campaign pamphlets. On the wall under the windows is a large campaign poster with the words "DIPIETRO-HE MAKES A DIFFERENCE." Directly across from the machines is a newer folding table and chairs. Above the chairs is a large clock on the wall with the hands exposed. Behind the table are several signs which read "Polling Place" and some plastic American flags. It is 5:30 AM March 21, 1974.

Frank Bolsic enters, whistling. He is dressed in a synthetic brown suit and blue and white striped short-sleeved polyester shirt, despite the forty degree March temperature. His wide beige tie is neatly set at his neck except for the last stage of the process. The larger and longer portion of the tie is pulled over the knot instead of through it, where it hangs to just above his navel. He walks to the windows, and pulls back the dusty drapes to reveal whatever light he can, then begins to open the folding chairs, an action he has performed hundreds of times before. Enter Cindi Wong and Sheila, carrying a large cardboard box. Bolsic turns as they enter.

BOLSIC: *(smiling)* Good Morning, girls!
SHELIA: What's so good about it?
CINDI: Hi Frank. Where do you want this?
BOLSIC: You can set it in the corner over there for now, Cindi.
They move to the far corner of the room, laboring with the box.
Cindi is Chinese, in her late thirties with a quiet smile. She wears a large button, somewhat worn, on her wool sweater which reads "DEMOCRATIC

JUDGE." *Although her trim figure complements her soft face and longish black hair which is pulled back, she wears no make-up and the years of being a single mother seem to have taken a toll on her.*

They place the box on the floor. Sheila extends herself with her hands on the small of her back, just above her large hips and sighs to the wall, "Ah Sheesh." She is a large woman but no one has ever mentioned that fact to her. She wears a two piece floral double-knit outfit with large plastic earrings that match the pattern of her dress. She is five or six inches taller than Cindi without considering the scale of her coiffure, which untraditionally, has been done in mid-week in anticipation of the day's activities, along with her excessive make-up. Cindi removes a coffee pot from the box and begins setting it up.

SHEILA: Sweet rolls, Frank?

BOLSIC: *(studying the list)* In the box on the table, She.

She removes her Democratic Judge button from her purse, applies it in the manner of a corsage and proceeds to open the two boxes of sweet rolls. Cindi finishes scooping coffee into the antiquated percolator and soon the room begins to take on the scent of politics.

Enter the Assistant, left, carrying Bolsic's briefcase. He wears a coat and tie, but is without purpose or station in life, condemned to remain on the periphery. He removes lip balm from his pocket and applies it excessively.

ASSISTANT: I brought your briefcase in, Frank.

BOLSIC: So I see. The two women say nothing.

ASSISTANT: Hi, Cindi!

CINDI: Good morning, Herb.

ASSISTANT: What's new, She? *(Sheila says nothing and continues to set up the supplies for the day.)* I saw you at the fundraiser at the Bismark last week. I didn't want to disturb you because you were talking to Charlie Marks. How's he doing? *(Sheila looks up debating whether to speak to the Assistant.)*

SHEILA: The Mexicans are taking over his ward and his wife's diabetes is getting worse. Any other questions?

ASSISTANT: Take it easy, She, you must have had a rough night last night. *(She glowers at him. He gravitates to Cindi in the corner.)* How is your son doing, Cindi?

CINDI: *(smiling)* He took second place in a computer quiz for his whole school last week.

ASSISTANT: And he's only, what, a sophomore?

CINDI: Freshman.

ASSISTANT: Freshman! Holy Toledo! The kid's gonna be a rocket scientist.

CINDI: He wants to be a doctor.

ASSISTANT: Cind, only the best for you kid, that's all ya deserve.

CINDI: Herb your lips are bleeding.

ASSISTANT: Oh no Cind, its just cherry lip balm.

CINDI: Cherry lip balm?

A knock on the door and Bolsic looks up. A knock again.

BOLSIC: *(yelling)* It's open!

The four turn as Orland enters, carrying a briefcase. He may be twenty-three years of age and wears a raincoat over a corduroy sport jacket, a faded denim shirt and jeans. His confusion stems less from the possibility that he's lost than from the inference as soon as he enters that he is an unwelcome guest.

ORLAND: Excuse me, is this the fifty-sixth ward, thirteenth precinct?

BOLSIC: It sure is kid. Who are you?

ORLAND: *(straightening himself)* I'm a poll watcher.

BOLSIC: *(glancing at the Assistant)* Who sent you down here kid, Collins?

ORLAND: No sir, I don't know Mr. Collins.

BOLSIC: Are you a floater from downtown?

ORLAND: No, I don't think so.

BOLSIC: I don't get it, kid.

ORLAND: Get what sir?

BOLSIC: What I mean is, who are you with?

ORLAND: Oh, *(relaxing and beginning to smile)* I see what you mean. I'm a member of the independent organization of Louis Gunderson.

The tiny hairs on the back of Bolsic's neck begin to rise. He is not a man who is required to hold his temper often. As it is, he is momentarily speechless. The Assistant senses this and walks over to inspect the watcher.

ASSISTANT: *(looking at him as if he were an extra-terrestrial)* Are you kidding? Don't you realize where you are son? We don't need any help running this polling place. This is a Dipietro precinct. If I were you ...

BOLSIC: *(calmer and turning his irritation to his assistant)* What the hell kind of a way is that to treat a guest Herb? *(glancing at the poll watcher, gradually loosening up)* Kid gets up early in the morning to drive here from the suburbs, probably had a hell of a time finding the place, afraid they're going to steal his car and you're givin' him the third degree. There may not be any hope for you Herb. *(he extends his hand palm facing up)* How do you do son? I'm Frank Bolsic, precinct captain of the fifty-sixth ward, thirteenth precinct, regular Democratic organization.

ORLAND: How do you do, I'm pleased to meet you.

BOLSIC: *(turning to the two women)* This is Sheila and Cindi, our two girls. *(he winks at them)*

SHEILA: Hello.

CINDI: *(eyeing him and wondering)* Good morning.

BOLSIC: First campaign kid?

ORLAND: Yeah, I guess so.

BOLSIC: That's okay. Ya gotta start somewhere right? Everybody's entitled to participate. What are you, a college student?

ORLAND: Yes, sir.

BOLSIC: *(chuckling as he looks him over)* How did a nice kid like you end up working for a guy like Gunderson?

ORLAND: I'm sorry, Mr. Bolsic, I don't follow you.

BOLSIC: Frank, call me Frank, kid. Never mind. Take off your coat, its going to be a long day. Cindi, get the kid some coffee.

Orland moves to Cindi and the coffee pot and removes his coat. Cindi hands him the cup.

CINDI: We have sugar and cream in the box in the corner. I haven't had a chance to set it up yet.

ORLAND: This is fine thank you. It's cold out there.

Suddenly the doors fly open, left, and two men in leather jackets burst in waving open wallets. Orland spills his coffee but no one notices.

STATE'S ATTORNEYS: *(almost in unison)* Good morning! State's Attorney's Office! State's Attorney. We're here to check the machines! Good morning. State's Attorney! *(they move quickly to the back of the closed voting machines.)*

Bolsic stands arms crossed, smiling and shaking his head.

STATE'S ATTORNEY ONE: You got a reading, Earl?

STATE'S ATTORNEY TWO: She's covered with dirt. I'll have to scrape 'er. *(He pulls a small knife from his breast pocket.)*

STATE'S ATTORNEY ONE: Let 'er rip, Earl.

STATE'S ATTORNEY TWO: *(leans over momentarily in back of the machine)* This one's okay. *(he leaps to the back of the other machine)*

STATE'S ATTORNEY ONE: How about that one?

STATE'S ATTORNEY TWO: A-Okay. We're outta here. *(they prepare to depart)*

BOLSIC: *(to State's Attorney one)* Working hard son?

STATE'S ATTORNEY ONE: Oh, yes sir.

BOLSIC: Well, you asked them for a job, that's what they gave you. *(he chuckles)*

The attorneys look at each other and depart.

Orland looks frantically for napkins to clean up the spilled coffee. He finds them and begins to wipe the floor. Sheila looks at him.

SHEILA: Are you nervous?

ORLAND: *(wiping)* No,... I just. Who were those guys?

SHEILA: They're from the State's Attorney's Office. They have to check the machines before we open.

ORLAND: What do you mean "check the machines?"

SHEILA: To make sure, you know. That there are no votes on them before we start.

ORLAND: *(thoughtfully)* Oh, I see.

Bolsic is huddled with the Assistant, left, in the corner of the room. They are whispering. Their conversation ends as the watcher begins to look at the two of them. Cindi and Sheila are almost ready to open. The Assistant approaches Orland.

ASSISTANT: Listen kid, I'm sorry I was so hard on you. We all have a job to do right?

ORLAND: *(sitting at the small table, removing a legal pad from his briefcase)* Yeah, well I guess that's true, we do have a job to do.

ASSISTANT: *(reaching for the sweet rolls)* How about a sweet roll, son?

ORLAND: *(looking at the women)* Why don't you offer them to the ladies first?

The two women look at each other.

ASSISTANT: Oh, heh heh, they'll have time to eat. They gotta finish setting up first. I don't think we've met formally. I'm Mr. Calandra, the assistant precinct captain.

SHEILA: *(silently mouthing to Cindi)* Mr. Calandra!

ASSISTANT: What's your name son?

ORLAND: Jeffrey Orland.

ASSISTANT: *(taking a sweet roll and setting the box in front of the watcher)* Have you ever been a poll watcher before Jeffrey? Go ahead take one.

ORLAND: *(hesitates, then picks out a raspberry sweet roll)* No, that is, not in this type of situation, exactly.

ASSISTANT: I see, so you're a newcomer to the political process.

ORLAND: Oh, I don't know, I've been interested in the process since I was in high school.

ASSISTANT: Are you a student now, Jeff, or working or...

ORLAND: Yes, I'm at Northwestern.

ASSISTANT: *(eating the sweet roll)* Fantastic! What are you taking up?

ORLAND: Political science.

ASSISTANT: Political science! *(crumbs fly from his mouth)* Frank, we got a political science guy over here by me! Well, you're certainly in the right spot today kid. Did they tell you what to do? Do you understand your role?

ORLAND: I guess I'm supposed to mark off the various voters on this list as they come in, one column for Democrats and one for Republican.

ASSISTANT: You got it kid! Tell me, did they get everyone together in one spot this morning to give you your assignments or was that last night or how did they set that up? It must have been a big job.

ORLAND: You're right. I never realized how much work goes into organizing an election day before. We all met this morning at South End Headquarters ...

ASSISTANT: Where is that? Over on Pershing.

ORLAND: No, on Ashland.

ASSISTANT: Oh Ashland, yeah, okay.

ORLAND: They gave us kind of a pep talk. It was sort of exciting. I got to meet some of the higher ups first hand.

ASSISTANT: It's fun, isn't it Jeff. You feel like you're really involved, like you're part of a team.

ORLAND: *(getting excited)* Exactly, I never knew it was like this.

ASSISTANT: So who did you get to meet *(he jabs him)* besides the good looking girls?

ORLAND: Well, the candidate wasn't there but I met Mr. Archer, who's the finance chairman and I met State Representative Childers and his wife, who's really a knock-out.

ASSISTANT: So I hear!

ORLAND: And John Fullerton was there, which surprised me because I thought he was a regular. *(Bolsic looks up from his voter list and stares out downstage. He removes a small notebook from his breast pocket and makes a notation.)*

ASSISTANT: *(animated)* Anybody else you remember, Jeff?

ORLAND: Not offhand. Anyway Mr. Bolsic was right, I had a tough time finding this place. It was dark and they don't have lights over the addresses on these buildings.

ASSISTANT: *(withdrawing, less animated)* You're right about that kid.

SHEILA: I think we're ready Frank.

BOLSIC: Good, it's about one minute to. Herb, get you're pamphlets and open the outer door on the way out.

ASSISTANT: Sure thing, Frank. *(he exits)*

DUNESHADOWS

Orland places his registration list to the left of the legal pad on top of the card table where he is sitting. There is a sense of anticipation in the room, as if a medical operation is about to commence. There is more light in the room now and the voting machines have been opened up. Each machine has a curtain hanging from a steel rod at its entry. Orland removes a pen from the inside pocket of his sportcoat and begins to study the list. His manner has become more business-like and Sheila, seated at a distance takes a long look at him. She is puzzled and unsure.

SHEILA: Were you canvassing in the neighborhood last month young man? *(Orland does not look up. She speaks louder.)* Young man.

ORLAND: *(he looks up)* Jeffrey, call me Jeffrey.

SHEILA: Jeffrey, did I see you canvassing in the neighborhood about a month ago?

ORLAND: No, I don't think so. I haven't spent a lot of time in the neighborhood so far, it must have been someone else.

SHEILA: I must be mistaken. Have you enjoyed your work so far?

ORLAND: Very much, ma'am. Chicago is such an interesting town politically. There are so many people from so many different kinds of backgrounds.

SHEILA: That's right, especially this ward. We got everyone. Irish, Italian, Chinese, colored, I mean…black. *(Orland says nothing)*

Herb enters left, beaming, helping an elderly woman.

ASSISTANT: Well, look who I found on her way in!

BOLSIC: Mrs. Calabrese, you've done it again!

SHEILA: *(to Orland)* That's Mrs. Calabrese. She's been the first voter in this place for years.

CINDI: Hello Mrs. Calabrese. You're up bright and early again.

MRS. C: So what am I gonna do, Cindi? Sit around the house and twiddle my thumbs? You got an Italian boy running here, I want to be the first one to vote for him.

SHEILA: You know the family don't you Mrs. C.

MRS. C: *(waving her hand)* Honey, when Giovanni Dipietro first went to work for Streets and San in 1934 he told me one day a son of his would be a big shot in the neighborhood. The only thing he didn't know then was which neighborhood, if you know what I mean. *(The others laugh. Orland looks at her and smiles. She sees him and walks toward the table where he sits.)* I don't believe I know this young man.

ORLAND: How do you do, my name is Jeffrey Orland.

MRS. C: Hello Mr. Jeffrey Orland, are you Frank's new assistant?

ASSISTANT: Oh no, Mrs. C., nothing like that, nothing at all. He's a

college student working for the guy running against Tommy.
(There is a sudden stillness in the air.)

MRS. C: What, my God, a Republican?

ORLAND: No, not that. Louis Gunderson is an Independant.

MRS. C: I see... independant of what?

ORLAND: Well, it's just the name of the movement.

MRS. C: A movement, what movement? There's only one movement, young man. The regulars are the movement here. You look like a nice boy, couldn't they find a place for you? Did you ask Mr. Collins? Frank, help this boy.

Bolsic stands with arms crossed looking at Orland.

ORLAND: *(quietly, measured)* Thank you, Mrs. Calabrese, but I don't need Mr. Bolsic's assistance.

MRS. C: What do you want? Do you want the colored and the Spanish and the rest of them *(Cindi glances away)* to take over?

Is that what you want? *(There is silence. She sighs.)* Oh well, *(looking at Bolsic)* you try, Frank, that's all you can do with young people, you try. *(She steps in front of Sheila)*

SHEILA: *(calling out)* Angelina Calabrese, 1844 West Hudson.

Mrs. C. takes a voter's card and enters the machine past the open curtain. The Assistant exits. Bolsic, who has been standing to her left during the conversation, deftly, in one motion, pulls the lever closing the curtain and positions himself where the corner of the curtain does not quite meet the side of the machine. Orland, who had been looking for Mrs. C's name on the roster, suddenly notices this and begins to stare at Bolsic with a blank expression. Cindi pours herself a cup of coffee. Sheila is busy with paperwork. Bolsic hovers until the woman is finished. She finally exits from the booth and drops her card into the large box on the table.

SHEILA: Thank you, Mrs. C.

MRS. C: You're welcome, Sheila. Good bye.

BOLSIC: Good bye, Angie, say hello to the family. *(She exits.)*

SHEILA: *(to Cindi)* She's a nice lady.

Enter a young man in work overalls, holding a lunch bucket.

BOLSIC: Hello, Bobby! *(He slaps him on the back)* How are they treating you over there?

THORESEN: Fine, Frank, fine. I came in early so I wouldn't be late to work. *(He steps up to the table.)*

CINDI: Robert Thoresen, 1528 West Colfax.

She hands him his card and Orland checks the roster for his name. The young man enters the booth and Bolsic takes up the same position. Orland puts his pen down waiting for the voter to emerge. He is out in seconds and deposits his card in the box.

THORESEN: So long, girls. Bye Frank.

BOLSIC: *(to no one in particular)* Kid's a bricklayer. *(calling after him)* Don't lay too many today, Bobby! *(he laughs heartily)*

ORLAND: Mr. Bolsic, can I speak with you for a moment?

BOLSIC: *(still chuckling)* Sure, kid, what can I do for you?

ORLAND: Well it's kind of difficult for me to... but...

BOLSIC: What is it, kid, you feeling ok?

ORLAND: Yes, fine thank you. Do you think that you could please not stand so close to the voters inside the booth, while they're voting? *(Sheila and Cindi put down their pens, Sheila's mouth is agape. Cindi is studying Orland more intently than ever. Bolsic digests the question and is no longer chuckling but his smile is still there.)*

BOLSIC: Was I standing too close for you, kid? Was I doing that?

ORLAND: Well it looked like it from here but it might have been the angle from where I was sitting.

BOLSIC: By the book kid, it's the only way to go. Ya gotta go by the rules or you got chaos, right?

ORLAND: I wasn't...

BOLSIC: *(putting his hand on Orland's shoulder)* Am I right kid?

ORLAND: You're right.

BOLSIC: *(with as much sincerity as he is capable of)* A woman like Mrs. C., kid, she could fall. I've never had an accident in my precinct but there's always a first time. We can't be too careful, am I right?

ORLAND: Well, anyway.

BOLSIC: *(Sharply)* Cindi, get me a cup of coffee will ya? *(to Orland)* Keep your eye on your roster. We usually get pretty busy around this time.

(FADE)

SCENE TWO - LATE MORNING

The pace has slowed considerably. The two women have finished their initial paperwork and are sitting, somewhat bored. Cindi is reading a book. Bolsic and the Assistant have gone to pick up some voters. Orland is up out of his chair walking around the room. Sheila is doing her nails and watching him.

SHEILA: You know, Jeffrey, I think it was wrong for you to speak to Frank that way before.

ORLAND: What do you mean, Sheila?

SHEILA: You know, when you were complaining about his helping the voters.

ORLAND: Oh that. Well, I just thought I should say something.

SHEILA: Why? Frank Bolsic has been running this place for years. He knows the rules. This place runs as smooth as any in the city and his numbers are as good as any precinct in the city or the county. I don't want you to feel bad when I tell you this. You are a nice boy, a smart boy. But you can't really come in here in your first election working for Mr. Louie Nobody and start telling Frank how to run this place. He has been very nice to you. Sometimes he's not so nice. In some of the other wards they wouldn't even give you a place to sit. I've seen it in other elections. Those people aren't as nice as we are. *(Cindi has put her book down and is listening to the other election judge.)*

ORLAND: Let me ask you something Sheila, do you live in this housing project?

SHEILA: What are ya's crazy? Of course not and neither do you.

ORLAND: Exactly, so what position are you or I really in to speak to the people in this ward who don't have the power or the access to the people who do especially if they have a problem or they want to get something done.

SHEILA: What are you talking about power and access? I just made a comment about your interfering with the way Frank runs this place.

ORLAND: The way Frank runs this place is one of the reasons why I'm here working for Louis Gunderson. I know it is comfortable for people like yourself in this ward and you have no complaints and you think the Mayor is the greatest guy around but your people are the ones in control. They've been in control for a long time. Mayor Daley has been the mayor for a long time and I don't see a situation where any candidate can ever defeat him. But the way the system exists now nobody else has a chance to get inside to change things.

SHEILA: Change? Is that what you want? What's to change? As long as the garbage is picked up and the streets are plowed and the city runs, what's wrong with that?

ORLAND: Cindi knows what I'm talking about.

CINDI: I know what you're talking about but I don't agree with you.

ORLAND: Why not?

CINDI: You're not married are you?

ORLAND: No.

CINDI: And you don't have any children do you?

ORLAND: No I don't.

CINDI: I do. I have a son who is the most important thing in my life to me. There are scholarships that are available to the regular organization and he's going to get one. I don't live in this housing project but I have relatives who do. I want my son to have it better financially than I have it. He's going to have it better and I'm willing to work for that. When I started with the organization I was an outsider, a real outsider. But I worked hard, I worked within the system. I still do but I still have my self respect. That's very important to Chinese people, face is important. So when I see someone come into the organization or groups demanding a status that I have worked hard for I take offense at that. All it takes to get what they want is hard work. If it's access to the mayor's office or contracts or even getting their street repaved it requires some effort, not just demands that they are entitled to it. You, you're in a different catagory. But I don't identify with you any more than with the others, your needs are not my needs. You don't live in my neighborhood. Candidates like yours come in with their liberal baloney and they think this city exists in an ethnic vacuum. They don't recognize or at least admit that how much you can get done for people in your ward or district has a lot to do with who you are — white, black, Asian or Hispanic, Irish, Italian, Polish or whatever.

ORLAND: I'm sitting here listening to you Cindi and the fact of the matter is that I agree with ninety-five percent of what you're saying but the picture you paint isn't an attractive one to me. Did you ever seriously consider that the Asian people in this city could have candidates of their own? Is it too much to envision Chinese and Korean people working with the same priorities? I would imagine you were very much an outsider when you joined the organization but how far inside can you realistically go? The whole system stinks for those who don't have access.

CINDI: And Louis Gunderson is going to change all that? He offers less to my family or my people than the organization does now. There are problems in this ward in getting a consensus even among Chinese. There are older people who have never actually left the neighborhood since they arrived in Chicago. At least the regular organization offers consistency. It is something we can depend on because it has been that way and it's going to be that way for a long time.

ORLAND: You want to depend on somebody like Frank Bolsic, is that what you're telling me?

(Sheila, who has been listening, now glares at Orland.)

CINDI: He's not so bad. I've seen worse. He knows a lot more about winning in the ward than your people, I can guarantee you that. Besides most of the voters know who Dipietro is. Your candidate is really a poor choice to run in a place like this, he looks like a meek little man.

SHEILA: He's a poor choice to run anyplace, Cindi.

ORLAND: *(slowly grinning)* Are you saying he lacks charisma?
(The two women laugh.)

SHEILA: *(shaking her head)* Why don't you do yourself a favor and sign on with the regulars, Jeffrey? A kid like you could go far even if you don't live in the city. *(she smiles)* Besides you get to meet pretty girls.

ORLAND: But Sheila, I've had that opportunity this morning anyway and I'm still an Independant.

SHEILA: Cind, will you listen to this kid? He's gonna make us forget what we're doin' here.

CINDI: *(to Orland)* Still an Independant, still not listening.

ORLAND: Saving face.

CINDI: You know a lot about politics for someone in his first election.

ORLAND: Well, thanks Cindi. I guess I just like to watch people and listen to what they have to say. I never thought I'd actually be involved in a campaign.

CINDI: Why not?

ORLAND: I don't know. It's a lot different than what you see on TV. It has more to do with ringing doorbells (both women laugh) than I thought.

CINDI: Have you ever thought about running for office yourself?

ORLAND: Me? No, not really. Why do you ask?

CINDI: Well, I'll tell you something that's true not just in politics but in life, Jeffrey. You may find yourself working against someone like Frank or me or Sheila in a campaign like this but if you stick around you will end up working with us at one point or another.

ORLAND: I could never imagine being a regular.

CINDI: Never is not a good word to use in this business. But I don't mean it that way. If you work in government you have to try to get things done and you can't do it by yourself. You need cooperation. If you offend people, especially on first impression, it is much more difficult to get things done. Of course you have to believe in the process in the first place in order to succeed.

ORLAND: I'm not sure that I do.

CINDI: A lot of people don't, or don't think about it.

ORLAND: Have you ever run for office, Cindi?

CINDI: No. I'm more concerned with raising my son and getting to work everyday.

ORLAND: What department do you work in?

CINDI: Strategic planning.

ORLAND: Your department chief keeps talking about razing all the old buildings, especially in the north loop.

CINDI: It won't happen. At least for the time being. There are too many buildings with historical significance. And too many people with competing interests.

ORLAND: *(smiling slightly)* Maybe those people should learn to cooperate. Anyway, I hope you're right. Sitting in the balcony and eating popcorn in those old theaters is an important childhood experience.

SHEILA: There's rats in those theaters.

ORLAND: That makes it more exciting.

Enter John Dare, a black man in his late fifties, wearing an old gray suit and slouching. With the exception of his diamond pinkie ring, his outward appearance is tired and resigned.

DARE: Hey girls, what's up?

SHEILA: Hi, John.

CINDI: Looking for Frank, John?

DARE: Cindi you read my mind, just like you always do.

CINDI: He went over to fourteen with Herb but he should be back before lunch. Any problems?

DARE: No, we're lookin' real good. I got a few transport hangups on the east side but my people are all producin'. *(Looking at Orland)* Don't tell me we finally got us a real Republican election judge.

ORLAND: No, I'm not a judge.

SHEILA: He's a poll watcher for Louie Gunderson.

DARE: Gunderson? *(He waves his hand in disgust.)*

CINDI: How's your wife, John?

DARE: She's not too good right now, Cindi, but I appreciate your askin'. She's havin' problems keeping her water. She back over at County so I been goin' over in the evenings. They ought to do somethin' about that place. They keep stealin' her money. I leave her a little so she can get her newspaper and ladies things but they come in when she's sleepin' and find it.

ORLAND: They're talking about building a new hospital.

DARE: Mister, they bin talkin' about that for years. That ain't never goin' to happen. The place is goin' be standing when you as old as I am.

ORLAND: Maybe, but they say it's really going to happen this time. They say they're going to get state funding and the county won't have to pay more than ten percent.

DARE: State funding! You think those people down there care about those poor people in County? They just as soon bomb that place before they gave it any more money way I see it.

ORLAND: That's not the way Gunderson sees it.

DARE: Gunderson ain't never been to that place. If he ever does come by I'd be happy just to show him around. Shoot, little fellow like that, he might get stepped on if he tried to go inside *(heh heh)*.

CINDI: Why don't you stick around, John. They should be back in just a little while.

DARE: Naw, I think I'll take a ride and see how things are doin' on Ashland but I'll be back before lunch. Tell Frank I'll see him then.

(He exits)

SHEILA: *(to Orland)* That's John Dare. He runs our colored vote.

ORLAND: He runs it?

SHEILA: Yeah, Frank pretty much lets him do his own thing. He's a good producer.

ORLAND: What percentage of this precinct is black?

SHEILA: *(unsure of Orland's direction)* I don't know, it varies. We got a hard enough time keeping them registered at the right address.

ORLAND: I get the feeling he's been doing this for a long time.

SHEILA: He has. He and his wife are still here but his children are all grown up and live outside the ward.

ORLAND: He must have younger people who work with him.

SHEILA: Why, *(only half-kidding)* you interested in working with him?

ORLAND: *(smiles at her)* No, Sheila.

Enter Allen Wong. He is fourteen and taller than his mother. He wears a white cotton shirt, jeans and carries his school books. Cindi's face brightens when she sees him and he walks toward her.

ALLEN: Hi mom.

CINDI: Hi honey, did you eat before you came over?

ALLEN: No, I didn't have time. I was finishing a program and I have to get back for physics in an hour.

CINDI: *(reaching in back of her)* Take a sweet roll. All we have left are apple and cherry.

SHEILA: Hi Allen, you get taller every election!

(They laugh. Allen looks at Orland.)

CINDI: *(beaming)* This is my son, Allen. Allen this is Jeffrey Orland.

ALLEN: How do you do?

ORLAND: Hi Allen, I heard you're a computer whiz.

ALLEN: No, I'm just a hacker.

ORLAND: That's not what I hear. Do they have a computer club at your school?

ALLEN: They're trying to get one started but they don't have any money for it right now. Me and another Chinese kid are trying to raise money from a restaurant in our neighborhood to get it started.

ORLAND: I think that's a great idea, Allen. *(taking out his wallet)* Please allow me to contribute toward your club.

CINDI: Oh, you don't have to do that.

ORLAND: I know I don't have to but I'd like to. *(He hands a five dollar bill to Allen.)*

ALLEN: Thank you very much Mr. Orland.

ORLAND: That's okay. Good luck to you.

Allen walks behind the table where his mother is sitting and they talk quietly for a minute. Allen finishes one sweet roll and takes another from the box and puts it in his book bag. She kisses him and says something audible in Chinese. He heads for the door and waves to the others.

ALLEN: Goodbye, nice to meet you Mr. Orland.

ORLAND: So long, Allen.

SHEILA: Take care, kid.

Just as he is about to exit the door opens and Bolsic and the Assistant enter. Bolsic looks at Allen for a second trying to recognize him.

ALLEN: Hi Mr. Bolsic... I'm Allen Wong remember?

BOLSIC: Oh sure, kid, how are ya? No school today?

ALLEN: I'm on my lunch hour.

BOLSIC: Well it's good to see ya kid. Geez, you're gettin' big! *(calling out)* Cindi, for cryin' out loud, the kid's bigger than Herb already. So long Allen.

Allen exits. Bolsic and the Assistant speak inaudibly to each other as they enter the room. Orland is studying his roster.

BOLSIC: Where we at, She?

(Sheila hands him her clipboard and he studies it.) What's the deal on the east side?

SHEILA: I don't know. John Dare was here and he said he had some transport problems.

BOLSIC: Is he coming back?

SHEILA: Yeah, he said he was coming back before lunch.

BOLSIC: *(looks at the overhead clock)* It's almost noon now. Have you girls eaten?

SHEILA: No, not yet.

BOLSIC: Herb, take their orders and see if you can find out where Dare is.

(The Assistant takes a pencil from behind his ear and walks toward the two women. Bolsic sits with Sheila's clipboard and begins writing. The Assistant spends a moment talking to the women and writing before he approaches Orland. He descends to one knee as Orland looks up from his roster.)

ASSISTANT: *(whispering, almost with pain)* Can I get you a sandwich, son?

ORLAND: No thanks, I'll get something later.

ASSISTANT: C'mon kid, we always order together here. *(he emits sorrow)* Ya can't eat sweet rolls all day, for cryin' out loud.

ORLAND: Well I, sure. Where are you going?

ASSISTANT: It's just a place down the street.

ORLAND: *(taking his wallet out again)* Let's see here...

ASSISTANT: *(already shaking his head)* It's okay kid. It's on the house. We'll take care of everything. What do you think, corned beef, a hamburger, roast beef, some french fries?

ORLAND: *(thinking a moment)* Roast beef is fine, with fries, as long as you're going already.

ASSISTANT: A little mayo on the side, son? and a coke?

ORLAND: Sure, why not.

(The Assistant finishes writing and tears the sheet from the pad. He winks at Orland.)

ASSISTANT: Back in no time, kid. You're gonna love this sandwich.

(As he rises to his feet John Dare enters and Bolsic looks up.)

BOLSIC: Well, look who finally showed up.

DARE: What do you mean finally showed up? I was here before, Frank. I was looking for you.

BOLSIC: You were looking for me, John? That's fortunate because I was looking for you too. I was also looking for half of fourteen hundred West Carlton. Have you seen them, John?

DARE: Frank, it ain't half a block. I told Sheila I had some transport problems.

BOLSIC: John, transport problems we can deal with but if your flunkies aren't producing that's another story.

DARE: I'm producing, Frank. You know my people are late voters. It's always been that way.

BOLSIC: Late voters. That's being charitable, John. Half of them don't even get up until noon. *(He winks at Sheila. Orland is watching him.)*

DUNESHADOWS

How long have you been in the organization, John?

DARE: As long as you, Frank. Longer even.

BOLSIC: And how old are you, John.

DARE: Sixty-seven... sixty-eight.

BOLSIC: Aren't you sure?

DARE: Today is my birthday.

BOLSIC: *(startled)* Today is your birthday? Well, happy birthday, John, you didn't even tell us! *(Dare says nothing.)* I just wanted to congratulate you, John, that's all. A man only has a birthday once a year. Now think for a minute, John. What is it, sixty-seven or sixty-eight?

DARE: Sixty-eight.

BOLSIC: There, I knew you could do it. Now tell me John, if you can remember how old you are how come you can't remember your fellow citizens on Carlton. The ones that aren't here, that don't work, that haven't voted and are hurting my numbers?

DARE: It ain't like that, Frank. I told Collins that I was havin' some problems earlier and that Gunderson had his people all over that street sayin' all kinds a shit and that I needed some help.

BOLSIC: You need help alright, John, but that's not the kind of help I'm talkin' about. Now what I think you ought to do is to get your black ass over there and see if you can find those people and get them in here before six o'clock because if you don't it'll be the last time you do any work in this ward, I don't care how long you been ringin' doorbells. *(Turning to the Assistant.)* Herb, go get me a beef with the works and a chocolate malted. *(The Assistant exits hurriedly. Calling out after him.)* And make sure he melts the goddamned cheese!

(FADE)

SCENE THREE 1:30 P.M.

Bolsic is sitting on one of the tables telling a canvassing story to Cindi, Sheila, Orland and the Assistant.

BOLSIC: ...so an old Chinese broad opens the door and I tell her who I am. She doesn't understand and calls her old man. He comes to the door and I start to give him the word about our boy but I don't think I'm getting through so I figure I'll go to the registry and I sez, "What's your name pal?" He says, "Fuck Louie!" *(Sheila and Herb laugh)* I'm trying to keep a straight face and he says it again. Fuck Louie. By this time I'm losing it so I give him a flyer, slap him on the back and tell him I couldn't agree with you more. *(more laughter)* I figure he's a walk on and don't think twice about it. I'm having coffee two hours later, checking the register and I'll be goddamned if I don't find him! His name really is Fuck Louie. *(frowning a bit)* Cindi has he shown yet?

CINDI: *(stonefaced, cold)* No, Frank.

Orland looks at her and imperceptively shakes his head.

ASSISTANT: Frank, these guys are always coming out of the woodwork. Who gives a shit if we get the name right or not as long as they show?

BOLSIC: Herb, we got a scientist here. The kid marks a good sheet. He gives a shit, and so do I. Get over there and see if you can find him.

Assistant departs. John Dare enters.

BOLSIC: Well, look who dusted off his ass to come callin' again!

DARE: Frank, I gotta talk to you.

BOLSIC: You didn't want to talk to me an hour ago. You didn't want to talk to me when I sent Herb looking for half of 1400 Harper cuz they hadn't gotten up yet.

DARE: Frank...

BOLSIC: But now you're here and I don't even need you and you probably got your hand out again.

DARE: What do you mean again?

BOLSIC: Let me ask you something, John. How long you been in the game? How long you been telling us what a good job you're doing for the boys downtown?

DARE: A lotta years, Frank?

BOLSIC: How many years?

DARE: Since '41.

BOLSIC: Well, if you started in '41 how many elections does that make? *(Orland puts his clipboard down, there is a nervous silence)* Do you understand what I asked you, John?

(Cindi begins to recheck her figures.)

SHEILA: What difference does it make, Frank? Come on we got work to do.

BOLSIC: Wait a minute, Sheila, I just asked the man a simple question. There's nothing to be nervous about, John. Okay maybe that one's too tough, here's an easy one. How many of those has the organization lost?

DARE: Well, none really since '59.

BOLSIC: Right and it's going to stay that way.

DARE: Frank, can we talk in the other room now?

BOLSIC: Of course, John, it's the least I can do for you on your

DUNESHADOWS 75

birthday. Right away. *(Dare exits right into the small side room)* Herb, call Collins for me when he gets back.

He follows Dare. Orland gazes curiously toward the side room. After a minute or two the two voices are audible.

ORLAND: What are they talking about, Sheila?

SHEILA: Money.

The voices rise. Bolsic is pounding on the table. Orland is staring at the door, the others do not pay attention. The voices descend. Enter a Chinese man, perhaps late sixties with an air of dignity and a reserved purpose. He is dressed in a worn coat and tie, accompanied by his wife, who is unsure. They move slowly toward Cindi.

CINDI: Good afternoon, may I have your name please.

VOTER: *(slowly, quietly but firmly)* Fouk Louie *(he rhymes Fouk with Duke. Orland looks up. Sheila glances up but says nothing)*

CINDI: And your address, sir?

VOTER: 1834 Carson. *(He has trouble with the street name and begins to speak Chinese with Cindi as each smiles at the other.)*

CINDI: Fouk Louie, 1834 Carson Avenue. *(Cindi directs him to the booth and provides instructions. The man smiles and says something to her. The wife waits outside the curtain. Cindi returns to her seat and her paperwork.)*

ORLAND: What did he say?

CINDI: *(pauses momentarily, then exhales)* He said this was his first opportunity to vote in his new homeland and he was very proud to have that honor.

Orland glances at the booth, then gazes back at Cindi. He says nothing but smiles slightly.

ORLAND: Were you born here Cindi?

CINDI: I was born on the ship that brought my parents to this country.

ORLAND: Really?

CINDI: What about you?

ORLAND: I'm not from this area originally. I was born back east.

CINDI: What state?

ORLAND: Connecticut

CINDI: You don't look like you're from Connecticut.

The curtain opens and the man exits, smiling. As he begins to bid good-bye to Cindi with a wave of his hand the side door simultaneously opens and Dare enters but says nothing. As Bolsic enters the main room he calls out,

"5:30" to Dare. Dare exits. Bolsic sees the Chinese man in front of him. The serious expression on his face changes to a smile as he nods. The voter continues to smile and with a wave of his hand exits with his wife.

BOLSIC: *(to Orland)* Well son, I hope you're learning something here today.

ORLAND: Oh yes sir, it's been very educational.

BOLSIC: Tell me kid, why are you here, really?

ORLAND: I told you, I'm from Gunderson's campaign.

BOLSIC: *(sizing him up again)* Yeah, maybe. But where you going to go with a mope like that? You gotta look at the big picture, kid. You gotta think about yourself. You see this town is just like Hollywood, you get caught with a couple of losers right in a row and nobody wants to give you the time of day.

ORLAND: I guess I got a lot to learn.

BOLSIC: You think I knew who the hell these guys were when I got started? You think I knew what the hell the county assessor was? You listen to people. You get in the middle of conversations and you keep your mouth shut. You find out things. You learn who's screwing who and when you think you know something you send out feelers. You look at the neighborhoods. You see who has the Polish, the Irish, the Jews. You look where the jobs are. You look at the young people, especially the sons of the guys who control the Park District, Streets and San, Inspectional Services. The families who are close to the man on Five. They're the ones who are going to get the nod sooner or later, the kids your age. It's a well oiled machine and they're the future parts. I tell you this because your a bright kid and I don't like to see talent wasted. If ya don't got it there's no puttin' it there but you can smell it, kid. After all, *(he laughs)* you found this god-forsaken stinkhole. *(Laughing)*

ORLAND: What happens Mr. Bolsic, if it doesn't go that way?
(Sheila rolls her eyes. Cindi looks at Bolsic.)

BOLSIC: What way? I lost ya kid, what do ya mean?

ORLAND: What happens if the future of the city and county is determined by something other than those relationships you were talking about? What if the machine fails? These guys aren't going to live forever.

BOLSIC: Kid, I'm not stupid, of course they're not but the system is there. Too many people got too much to lose to let it fall apart. There are problems sure. The colored and the Spanish are starting to get way out of line. Maybe we ought to give them a little more as long as they understand where it's all coming from. But the power of the thing, the control of the thing is always going to be in people like us.

ORLAND: Like me or like you?

BOLSIC: *(taken back momentarily)* You think you're better than me, kid? You think because you drive in here from the suburbs and drive out at six o'clock something's going to change? Your people have no clout. You can't elect some schmuck because he gets on TV and cries about rats in the projects. Those people aren't part of it. I'm tryin' to do you a favor, kid, I'm tryin' to help you out.

ORLAND: Are you offering me a part of it?

BOLSIC: *(laughs)* Maybe, if you're willing to work, because I'll tell you something. Politics takes more goddamned hard work than anything else but it pays off better than anything else. *(He winks at him.)*

ORLAND: Gunderson doesn't believe in payoffs.

BOLSIC: He doesn't, huh? Let me tell you something kid, there are only two kinds of people in this business, thieves and whores.

ORLAND: Which one are you, Frank? *(Sheila scowls.)*

BOLSIC: *(laughing)* Ha ha, I'll give you this, kid. Ya got balls.

ORLAND: *(curious)* How did you get started, Frank?

BOLSIC: My old man was in it, when he was sober.

ORLAND: Who was he with?

BOLSIC: Jack Aintree.

ORLAND: *(surprised)* Yeah?

BOLSIC: You know about Aintree, huh?

ORLAND: I uh, I read about him.

BOLSIC: Read about him? Where at Northwestern? Ha! Ha! Let me tell ya a story about Jack, kid. One of his constituents got into an accident years ago. Bad accident. He was drivin' a milk wagon on Ashland and got hit from behind by a streetcar. Threw him forward onto the cobblestones. Busted his head open. Real messy. The guy died in the hospital a couple hours later. His wife and nine kids don't know what the hell hit 'em. Jewish family. So they hire Clarence Darrow to sue the hell out of the City, figures right? *(He waves his hand)* True story, kid, I'm not lying. So the Captain, that's what a lot of us called Jack, he gets wind of this lawsuit and he pulls Darrow aside one day and he tells him to go easy on this thing because it don't sound too good for the city and he gives Darrow some crap about a conflict of interest because Darrow used to be a city lawyer or something. Anyway, the next thing you know Darrow gives the case to some kid in his office and they end up settling the thing for peanuts. But the Captain makes a mental note to remember this family because he figures they're owed, right? Well, the kids quit school and go to work, the widow buys a boarding house somewhere on the west side with the settlement money. One of her sons goes into the machinery business. The kid quit school in fifth grade but he's a natural with machinery, you follow me? Anyway a couple years pass and all of a sudden the war is on. You know which war I'm talking about, kid?

(He winks.)

ORLAND: Yeah Frank, I know. The last one we won.

BOLSIC: Anyway, the Captain is serving Uncle of course, but he makes a connection in the Army Supply Office. Except he don't say nothing to this machinery guy. He lets the government people approach this guy on their own but he makes it worth their while. *(He winks)* This guy makes a deal with the Feds and figures he did it on his own. He and his partners pulled a million bucks from Uncle Sam during the war from this deal and let me tell you something kid, that's still good money. The point is the Captain had vision. He knew how to get from one point to another without steppin on too many toes. That's classic politics, kid.

ORLAND: That's Chicago politics.

BOLSIC: No kid, it's like that everywhere, we're just not ashamed to tell it like it is around here.

ORLAND: Maybe this machinery guy just worked his butt off and took advantage of what life dealt him.

BOLSIC: Yeah, well like I said. This guy was a natural. I met him once. He told me a story that happened before his old man was killed. He came home one day when the son was about nine and complained to the kid's mother that business was no good and that they'd be better off if he took apart the milk wagon and sold the parts.

ORLAND: So what happened?

BOLSIC: The kid went downstairs… you know they used to have those walkups where the family lived on top and the horses were kept below… the kid went downstairs when they were sleeping and took the goddamn wagon apart. Nine years old! *(laughing)* The old man got up the next morning and couldn't believe it. Probably beat the crap out of 'em too. Anyway, you're right kid, that guy loved to work. He loved to get up in the morning and get his hands dirty. But it takes more than hard work to win in this town. You need influence.

ORLAND: And that's where people like you come in.

BOLSIC: Kid, I provide a service. Where do you think the term public servant came from?

ORLAND: I must have been mistaken. I thought it was the Greeks.

BOLSIC: Greeks? What Greeks? There are no Greeks in my ward, they're all north and west. Ha! Ha!

ORLAND: I guess the business has been pretty good to you, Frank.

BOLSIC: I deserve it, kid. You gotta kiss a lot of ass in this city to get anywhere and you gotta be able to size people up. You can't back losers kid, and I never seen a worse excuse for a candidate than Louie Gunderson.

ORLAND: So I figure you got me sized up too, right Frank?

BOLSIC: Well see kid, I been wrong once or twice before.

There is a momentary silence as Orland looks at Bolsic.

SHEILA: Do you think the candidate will come by, Frank?

BOLSIC: *(turning away from Orland)* Sure he will, She, a little later probably.

SHEILA: I hope so. I seen him at the fundraiser but didn't say nothin'. They say his kid brother has been campaigning with him. He's only what… fourteen or fifteen.

CINDI: He's the same age as my son.

BOLSIC: That kid brother is gonna break a lotta hearts.

SHEILA: That's what they say, Frank.

BOLSIC: They hit the north side first today but they'll show. My candidates always do.

ORLAND: You know Frank, I don't disagree with half of what you say.

BOLSIC: It's always gonna be that way. The people change but the business doesn't.

ORLAND: This really is a business to you isn't it? But you have a city job don't you?

BOLSIC: Of course I do, I told ya I ain't stupid, kid, but this is part of my job just like everyone else. That's Chicago. It's the nature of the place. There's action here.

ORLAND: Yeah, "City on the Make."

BOLSIC: Nelson Algren! Now there's a great writer, kid.

ORLAND: Yeah, but he left this city. Said he couldn't stand it anymore.

BOLSIC: It's not for everyone. But ya gotta understand it depends on your outlook. Me, I like the neighborhoods. I'm comfortable here. I ain't gonna be the mayor or the governor and I don't want to be. The people in this precinct know who they are. They get up in the morning, they go to work, most of them, they raise their kids, the men might stop for a quick one on the corner, they see to it the family stays together, they take care of the elderly, they live and they die.

ORLAND: But what about the future of this place? You have to have vision, you have to try to look down the road, you have to plan. The men who built this city thought that way but you don't see it anymore. It's every guy for himself.

BOLSIC: It's always been every guy for himself. You think the guys who built this city gave a shit about social causes? It was always power and money, always will be. Besides, Daley's a great mayor, he has vision. All those negroes who moved up here from the south, they all got a place to live. These projects, some of them in other wards not like this one, are shit houses. But these people don't even have to work if they don't want to. They got a place to live, they get money from the state, free medical care at County, what more could you ask for? If they aren't happy with it they ought to go out and get them a job just like everyone else.

ORLAND: They say they're not part of the political process.

BOLSIC: Who's stoppin' them from voting? I've never stopped any of them from comin' in here. We don't have problems like that in this precinct. I want as many registered as I can get and I want them all voting. Sometimes John's gotta drag them out of bed and they ain't sleepin', if you know what I mean, but my numbers are as good as any in the county.

ORLAND: They want positions of leadership in the Party.

BOLSIC: Let 'em work their way up like everyone else.

ORLAND: They don't want to wait that long.

BOLSIC: Then I say tough shit.

ORLAND: Maybe their time is coming.

BOLSIC: Not if I have anything to do with it.

Enter Tommy Watson. A young man in his late twenties wearing an elegant three piece suit.

BOLSIC: *(brightening)* Tommy! *(He moves forward to shake hands. The Assistant has been listening to Orland and Bolsic converse and now readies himself for a greeting, but remains unnoticed.)*

WATSON: Hello, Frank. How are you? Hi ya girls.

BOTH GIRLS: *(in unison)* Hi Tommy.

BOLSIC: Tommy, I was just speaking to our friend over here about people who work for a living.

WATSON: Ya got me, Frank.

BOLSIC: This is Jeffrey Orland, he's keeping an eye on us for Louie Gunderson.

WATSON: Gunderson! You must have taken a wrong turn pal. Anyway, I'm about to make your day better. *(In one motion he has removed a business card from his coat pocket and placed it in Orland's hand. The card reads, "Watson's New York Men's Shops Thomas Watson, President")* Come on into any location and fifteen percent off anything in the store. Give them the card. I mean anything, pal. What are you a student?

ORLAND: Yes, I am. I'm studying political science at Northwestern.

WATSON: Oh man, that's intense. I went to DePaul at night but I had to let it go. My first location was billing a million two and I figured let my accountant and lawyer earn what I'm payin' 'em. You look like a night student to me, Jeff. You got that half awake night student look. *(He winks.)*

ORLAND: *(quickly)* No, day school, day school.

WATSON: Oh well, maybe you've been partying like me. *(looking him over)* What do you got goin' there, kind of a young Ivy league thing?

ORLAND: My clothes? Oh… well, I'm on a tight budget.

WATSON: I got a dynamite credit plan, Jeff. You walk out of the place and you don't see me for two months. I got a fantastic single-breasted corduroy that's a little heavier than that but still comfortable.

ORLAND: Well, actually I prefer double-breasted suits.

WATSON: *(suddenly invigorated)* You want to go DB, pal? No problem. My buyer went nuts! I got DB coming out of my rectum! I'm givin' the stuff away. Are you north, Jeff?

ORLAND: Yeah.

WATSON: I'm in the center of the universe at Diversy and Halsted. I can be a little trendier there you know.

ORLAND: Yeah, I guess so.

WATSON: *(looking at Herb)* Herb, what the hell is that on your mouth?

ASSISTANT: *(distraught)* It's just lip balm, Tommy.

WATSON: Oh man, you look like you been eating pussy!

(Sheila and Bolsic laugh as Watson steps up to the table.)

SHEILA: Thomas Watson, 1921 Hillside… penthouse.

WATSON: Sheila, I'm gettin' special treatment again.

SHEILA: You deserve it Tommy. *(He enters the booth)*

BOLSIC: *(to Orland)* Here's a kid, lost both parents, pulled himself up, didn't ask nothin' from nobody and now he's drivin' a Cadillac. He's got what .. four or five stores now? *(calling out)* Tommy, where'd you just open?

WATSON: *(from inside the booth)* Palos!

BOLSIC: Palos! for crying out loud, the kid's twenty-eight years old and his fifth store is in Palos!

WATSON: *(exiting and handing his card to Sheila)* So long, girls. Stop by, Jeff, and look around.

ORLAND: Yeah, thanks. Nice to meet you.

BOLSIC: So long, Tommy. *(Watson exits)* A kid like that, he's a survivor. He don't worry about who's pullin' the strings, he just works his butt off. Every time I see him he's got a different chick on his arm.

SHEILA: He goes with Ralph Fuller's daughter now, Frank. I think he's hooked.

BOLSIC: Yeah? Ralph Fuller's kid? I think I seen her at the candidate's fundraiser about a month ago. She's a knockout.

Enter the Candidate and his Entourage, his Wife, the Alderman and the Kid. They are all well dressed including the Alderman's camel hair coat.

BOLSIC: Well, what do you know?

ALDERMAN: *(slowly, deliberately)* Hello, Frank, I hope it's been a good day.

BOLSIC: Thank you, alderman, it certainly has. We never have problems here.

ALDERMAN: I think you've met the candidate, Frank. This is his lovely wife, Patty, and his kid brother, Anthony.

(The Wife smiles, the Kid nods.)

BOLSIC: How do you do? *(to the Candidate)* You have a beautiful family, Mr. Dipietro.

CANDIDATE: Thank you, Frank. Who are these pretty ladies?

BOLSIC: *(turning)* These are our lovely girls, Cindi and Sheila.

CINDI: How do you do?

SHEILA: It's a pleasure to see you again. I was at the fundraiser last week and had a wonderful time.

CANDIDATE: Yes, of course, I knew we had met before.

ALDERMAN: *(moving to Orland)* Is this your new Assistant, Frank?

BOLSIC: No, this is Jeffrey Orland. He's here for the other candidate.

ALDERMAN: *(slight pause and a methodical opening of the hand palm up)* How do you do, son? I am Concento Marchese, Alderman of the 56th ward. If there is ever any way I can assist you please don't hesitate to call. *(Shakes his hand.)*

ORLAND: How do you do.

ALDERMAN: Have you worked in this ward before, Jeffrey?

ORLAND: No sir, I haven't. It's an interesting combination of people.

ALDERMAN: It certainly is, Jeffrey, and it's a pleasure to be able to assist people who are newcomers to this country, who rely on their elected officials and make Chicaga their new home.

ORLAND: I understand Alderman that you were the sponsor of the new sidewalk replacement ordinance that was recently passed.

ALDERMAN: Why, yes… yes I was.

ORLAND: Well from what I can gather in speaking to some of your constituents the program seems to be focusing almost entirely on the commercial property and not the residential. I even spoke to a senior citizen who broke her hip when she fell in front of her house.

ALDERMAN: I'm very sorry to hear that, Jeffrey. We try to allocate our resources in the most effective manner possible but sometimes there just isn't enough to go around.

ORLAND: As I understand it most of the other wards have placed a priority on residential areas.

ALDERMAN: Excuse me a moment, young man. *(turning to Frank)* Frank are you experiencing any difficulty on Hudson today? I understand there were some transport problems.

BOLSIC: *(smiling through gritted teeth)* No Alderman, not at this time. We had some minor difficulties this morning that we quickly took care of.

SHEILA: Would anyone like a cup of coffee or a sweet roll? We got plenty here.

CANDIDATE: *(to the Kid)* How about a sweet roll, Tony?

TONY: *(sheepishly)* Sure, okay.

He approaches Sheila who has opened the box for him.

SHEILA: Go ahead, Tony, take any one you'd like.

TONY: Thank you.

SHEILA: Sheila, call me Sheila.

TONY: Thank you, Sheila. *(He removes one.)*

SHEILA: Here let me give you a napkin. Sit down for a minute. You must be tired. How many precincts have you been to so far?

The others confer quietly to themselves.

TONY: A lot. I lost track. We met a lot of people in this campaign.

SHEILA: Yeah, well it's tough but it'll be worth it once the general election is over. I'll bet you'd rather be out chasing girls though. *(She winks at him. Tony is smiling sheepishly)* Or from what I hear they are chasing you.

TONY: I've taken a lot of time from school. I got some catching up to do.

SHEILA: Don't worry about that. There'll be plenty of time to do your school work.

CINDI: What school do you attend, Tony?

TONY: St. Francis, it's run by the Christian Brothers.

CINDI: Yes, I know. It's just two blocks from my son Allen's school.

TONY: You have a son who goes to Jensen?

CINDI: Yes, he's a a freshman.

TONY: They have a good basketball team.

CINDI: Yes, I guess they do.

BOLSIC: Sheila, you're filling the kid up with doughnuts. He's not going to be able to chase the girls at the party tonight.

SHEILA: He don't have to, Frank, they'll be chasing him.

ALDERMAN: *(looking at Sheila and Cindi)* You're very lucky Frank to have the valuable assistance of these two hard working gals.

BOLSIC: No question about it, Alderman, it's girls like these who are the backbone of the organization.

CANDIDATE: Well Alderman, shall we move on?

ALDERMAN: Yes, I'm - afraid so. *(quietly, to Bolsic, turning him aside)* Did you hear they got Coletti?

BOLSIC: *(he shrugs, barely audible)* That's what the guy gets for selling bad lettuce.

ALDERMAN: *(louder to the women)* It's a pleasure to see you again, girls. Keep up the good work. Come on, Tony. *(He turns to Orland)* Goodbye, son, it's nice to meet you. Remember, Jeff, there are no enemies in politics, only opponents.

ORLAND: Goodbye Alderman. *(He watches as the remainder of the entourage exits.)*

SHEILA: *(somewhat mesmerized)* He's a good lookin' kid ain't he?

BOLSIC: *(reaching for another sweet roll)* Stop robbin' the cradle, She, ha ha.

SHEILA: How'd he know about our troubles on Hudson?

BOLSIC: *(more serious)* I don't know but I'm going to find out.

CINDI: The candidate's wife is pretty. I don't think I've seen her before.

SHEILA: She don't like politics, that's gonna hurt him.

(FADE)

SCENE FOUR - 5:45 p.m.

A steady stream of Democratic voters have made their way through the basement and Orland has marked off each with his red marker. Three hundred forty of the three hundred sixty registered have voted but none of the five registered Republicans have shown up. In the back of Frank Bolsic's mind he is concerned about a problem that has occurred from time to time in years past - that the actual tally will have to be altered to produce numbers that are less lopsided in terms of Republican votes and the party's chosen candidates. Enter the Assistant with a young male voter.

BOLSIC: Hiya, Johnny, how's your mom?

JOHNNY: She's fine, Frank.

ASSISTANT: Johnny wants to talk to us outside.

BOLSIC: No problem, Johnny. Step outside into my office, heh heh! *(They exit)*

SHEILA: Jeffrey, you should listen to what Frank says about who you're associated with. He's been around for a long time.

ORLAND: Maybe that's part of the problem.

SHEILA: Problem? What problem? Listen to me you little shit I have half a mind to get Herb to throw you out of here right now.

CINDI: Sheila, come on, this is a polling place. He's got a right to be here. *(turning to Orland)* I wouldn't antagonize the way that you do, Jeffrey. In the first place it makes our job more difficult and I don't want to stay here any longer than I have to tonight. Secondly, it doesn't do any good. You're not going to change any minds around here with your ideas.

ORLAND: Not even yours, Cindi?

She looks at him. Enter Bolsic, the Assistant and the young voter.

BOLSIC: Okay She, Johnny is ready to vote, Republican.

SHEILA: John Brinkworth, 1618 Addison.

ORLAND: *(checks his roster)* I think that's the first one isn't he? *(no one replies)* I don't find him, Sheila. Is he an add on? *(He looks up, Sheila looks at Bolsic.)*

BOLSIC: Yeah kid, he's an add on. Your roster is just a photocopy of the master.

ORLAND: *(still checking)* Wait a minute. I got him as a Democrat.

BRINKWORTH: Well, I was but I changed my mind. *(He looks at Bolsic.)*

BOLSIC: *(quietly to Orland)* Jeff, the kid's embarrassed. Don't make him feel worse. The rest of his family are Democrats. He doesn't want the word to get out.

ORLAND: Frank, the kid isn't a registered Republican on my sheet. I'll let him go but I'm filing a protest.

BOLSIC: Fine, just let the kid vote. Okay Johnny.

The young man enters the booth as Herb exits. As Johnny votes Orland removes a red form from underneath his clipboard and begins writing. The young man exits from the booth and says nothing. In rapid succession three more young men enter.

CINDI: Edward Felachie, 1144 Cunningham, Republican. *(He steps toward the machine.)* Ryan Callahan, 1021 Alston, Republican. *(Cindi hands him a card and he steps in back of Felachie)* Philip Maderzek, 1444 Hudson, Republican.

Bolsic remains standing next to the machines nervously. As the first two are announced Orland says nothing. When Cindi announces Republican the third time Orland puts his clipboard down.

ORLAND: This has gone far enough.

BOLSIC: Kid, we got ten minutes before we close. I don't have time to argue with you now.

ORLAND: I'd like to see some real evidence that these voters who were previously Democrats are now legitimate Republicans.

BOLSIC: I can't accommodate you right now. I'm too busy.

ORLAND: These votes are improper.

BOLSIC: If you think we're breakin' the law call the cops.

Callahan is standing at the table in front of the two women watching the conversation.

ORLAND: *(to Bolsic)* Did you plan this so that it would coincide with closing?

BOLSIC: Kid, you're getting on my nerves again. Sheila, set the kid up. We don't have a lot of time.

Callahan enters the booth. Bolsic calls Herb aside.

BOLSIC: *(whispering)* Where we at?

ASSISTANT: 340 to 3. I got another few outside, Carl Jefferson and his kid, Mrs. Conroy, some others.

BOLSIC: We're gonna have a time problem. *(He steps away from the conversation and begins to glance furtively at the clock which reads 5:52.)* *(audibly)* Jeepers, I think your right, Herb, it's fast.

He pulls a chair up and stands on it as the Assistant holds it steady in preparation of turning back the hands. Orland sees this and steps out of his chair. John Dare returns and approaches Bolsic. Bolsic sees him and still standing on the chair reaches into his vest pocket, pulls out an envelope and tosses it to Dare, who is about five feet away.

BOLSIC: Here, John, it's all there.

Dare turns toward the wall and quickly counts the money inside. Orland watches him. He turns back to Bolsic.

ORLAND: Frank, what're you doin'?

BOLSIC: *(Trying to steady himself against the wall)* The clock, kid, it's fast. I'm just goin' to adjust it.

ORLAND: Frank ...

BOLSIC: *(on the chair)* I'm just adjusting the clock.

ORLAND: Frank...

BOLSIC: I'll be with you in a second kid.

ORLAND: Frank...

BOLSIC: One second, kid.

ORLAND: Get off the chair, Frank.

BOLSIC: *(stops what he is doing and turns to Orland)* What did you say to me?

The others including Dare are watching.

ORLAND: I told you to get off the chair.

BOLSIC: Who the hell do you think your talking too? I ought to throw you out of here right now. You come into my goddamned precinct and tell me what the hell I'm gonna do? I ought to bust your ass across this room and back to Kenilworth or whatever faggot suburb you came from.

ORLAND: *(measured, moving away from his table)* You do that, Frank. You bust my ass back to Kenilworth but get off the goddamn chair and take your hands off the motherfucking clock.

BOLSIC: *(pauses, looks at Orland, still on the chair, more measured, but seething)* You're through kid. You'll never be involved in the organization as long as I have anything to do with it. It's a serious mistake to burn your bridges in this business but you'll see that. Herb, hold the goddamned chair. *(He descends.)*

Orland produces a wallet from his inside pocket and displays it to Bolsic who is now in front of him.

ORLAND: You're under arrest, you have the right to remain silent, anything you say can and will be used against you. You have the right to an attorney. If you cannot afford one a lawyer will be appointed for you.

Cindi puts her hand to her mouth.

SHEILA: Oh my God!

The others are speechless. Orland reaches into his briefcase and withdraws a walkie-talkie.

ORLAND: Sixteen, I've got him. Come on in.

Bolsic is simply looking at Orland. The others say nothing. Dare, who has been standing in back of Orland drops the envelope with the money on the table in front of Orland. He and Bolsic momentarily look at each other but say nothing. Dare exits. A black uniformed officer enters and places handcuffs on Bolsic. Philip Maderzek is standing in front of the two women with his mouth open. Orland tosses his voter list into the briefcase and closes the latches. He looks up at the women.

ORLAND: Good evening, ladies, it was nice to meet you.

SHEILA: I don't believe it.

ORLAND: Why don't you believe it, Sheila? *(He looks at Maderzek standing there.)* You better take care of this guy.

The Assistant is staring at Orland.

ORLAND: Thanks for the sandwich, Herb.

Bolsic is led out and Orland follows him. Cindi slowly takes the voters card and calls out.

CINDI: *(in a strong voice)* Philip Maderzek, 1244 Dawson, Democrat.

(FADE)

EPILOGUE: 7:00 P.M.

An upstairs interview room at police headquarters. Orland and Tate, the other arresting officer, are seated around a wooden table with their feet up. Orland is smoking.

TATE: Do you think we can stick him?

ORLAND: *(distracted)* Who the fuck knows? Let the pointed shoe boys see what they can do with him.

TATE: Is Dare gonna show up in court?

ORLAND: *(pausing, looking directly at Tate)* I don't know Bob, you tell me. You tell me what's important to a guy like that.

TATE: You're asking the wrong guy.

ORLAND: *(laughs)* Come'on Bob, give me insight into the community. Let's have one of those discussions inter-departmental affairs is always suggesting take place.

TATE: Oh, *(animated)* you mean a rap session? Where I voice my concerns about racial polarity and you listen intently?

ORLAND: *(nodding)* And we develop a comprehensive community outreach plan.

TATE: Which we implement by face to face interaction.

ORLAND: You're not really interested in this shit, are you?

TATE: What shit?

ORLAND: Politics.

TATE: Hell no, I got enough to worry about. I got another goddamn child support garnishment to deal with.

ORLAND: You better be careful Bob. They're gonna grab your wheels next.

TATE: Not my baby! I'll be long gone by then. How did you get Dare in your pocket like that?

ORLAND: I dug up some crap from governmental affairs and I talked to some people. He was pretty receptive or else he was fed up enough to take a chance. I'm not sure he had anything to lose anyway.

TATE: Except maybe his life.

ORLAND: Maybe. But things are changing pretty quickly in that ward. I think they need him.

TATE: My father told me to stay the hell away from politics.

ORLAND: Why?

TATE: Well, he liked to gamble and he said there was no percentage in it for black folks.

ORLAND: There isn't. But you do anything long enough you're gonna make some headway and old John Dare has certainly been at it long enough.

TATE: So what's going to happen when it's over? Were they bullshitting or not?

ORLAND: I don't know. We'll see what Collins says.

TATE: He's a jag off.

ORLAND: So what?

TATE: So maybe you're playing with fire there, my boy.

ORLAND: I finish my master's degree this June. The department won't hassle me after that.

TATE: What you need are a few of those garnishments to make you more responsible.

ORLAND: Responsible? If you weren't such a stud you wouldn't have those problems.

TATE: I can't help it if the ladies can't keep their hands off.

ORLAND: Bullshit... *(they get up)* Turn the light off or I'll write you up.

TATE: You're already pulling rank on me and you aren't even there yet. *(They exit.)*

(CURTAIN)